What If . . . ?

Amazing Stories Selected by
MONICA HUGHES

Tundra Books

To Kate with love from Gran
– M.H.

Copyright © 1998 by Monica Hughes

Published in Canada by Tundra Books, McClelland & Stewart Young Readers,
481 University Avenue, Toronto, Ontario M5G 2E9

Published in the United States by Tundra Books of Northern New York,
P.O. Box 1030, Plattsburgh, New York 12901

Library of Congress Catalog Number: 98-60388

Canadian Cataloguing in Publication Data

Main entry under title:

What if – –? : amazing stories

ISBN 0-88776-458-4

1. Children's stories, Canadian (English).*   2. Fantastic fiction,
Canadian (English).*   3. Science fiction, Canadian (English).*
I.   Hughes, Monica, 1925–   .

PS8323.F3W42 1998   jC813′.087608054   C98-930681-X
PZ5.Wh 1998

We acknowledge the support of the Canada Council for the Arts for our
publishing program.

We acknowledge the financial support of the Government of Canada
through the Book Publishing Industry Development Program for our
publishing activities.

Printed and bound in Canada

  3 4 5 6   04 03 02 01 00

What If . . . ?

ACKNOWLEDGMENTS

Star-Seeing Night: Copyright © 1994 by Alice Major. First published in *On Spec*, Fall 1994.

The Stranger: Copyright © 1984, 1998 by Monica Hughes. Revised from story "Zone of Silence" appearing in *Out of Time* (Bodley Head, 1984).

Eternity Leave: Copyright © 1998 by Tim Wynne-Jones.

The Tunnel: Reprinted with permission of Margaret K. McElderry Books, an imprint of Simon & Schuster Children's Publishing Division from *Back of Beyond* by Sarah Ellis. Copyright © 1996 Sarah Ellis. Also "The Tunnel" from *Back of Beyond* Copyright © 1996 by Sarah Ellis. A Groundwood Book/Douglas & McIntyre.

Moon Maiden: Copyright © 1998 by Alison Baird.

A Wish Named Arnold: "A Wish Named Arnold" Copyright © 1987 by Charles de Lint. First appeared in *Spaceships and Spells* edited by Jane Yolen, Martin H. Greenberg and Charles Waugh (Harper & Row, 1987). Reprinted by permission of the author.

CONTENTS

FOREWORD

Monica Hughes

"What if . . .?" Words of wonder, words that lead the reader into a new story, into every kind of possibility. When I asked writers from across Canada if they had a story of either science fiction or fantasy for this anthology – something to amaze and delight the reader – I had no idea what might arrive in the mail. Would I be inundated with stories set on far frozen planets, with battles in space and threatening aliens? What I found in my mailbox, to my surprise and delight, were stories more of fantasy than "hard" science fiction, almost all of them, in one way or another, touching base right here on Earth.

And after all, why not? We inhabit a strange and splendid world, and stories about endangered species and a threatened environment, about visits from aliens – gentle or lonely, about witches and dinosaurs, as well as stories about young people discovering themselves and making critical choices are all every bit as exciting as *Star Wars*.

Perhaps it takes fantasy and science fiction to open our eyes to the wonders of Earth. It is "not about hiding things but about discovering things"; "the best way I know to tell the truth." Millions of children have grown up in cities, since the advent of modern street lighting, who have never seen the breathtaking splendor of the Milky Way blazing across the sky on a clear moonless night. Why? Because of light pollution. And every day taps run to make drinking water cold and shower water hot – this precious substance draining away unnoticed, unvalued – while poisons pour into our rivers and lakes.

The two poems in this collection are like bookends containing the varied stories within. They say, indirectly, as poems tend to, that our Earth, our sky, and our water are wonderful and irreplaceable. So let us enjoy, be amazed, and take care!

What if . . . the stars came out only once
in a thousand years?

STAR-SEEING NIGHT

Alice Major

Nikki, six years old, bundled
in her brother's coat, blinks away
sleep's slow sedative.

> *Will we see the moon? she asks.*
> *Maybe, if the clouds break soon enough,*
> *they tell her. Aren't you a lucky girl*
> *to see the stars?*

But moon and stars to her are mere
abstractions. She knows about them
as she knows elephants and sailing ships.
Has seen stars in photographs taken
high above the clouds' narcotic quilt
– jewels thrown savagely on black cloth
by some magnificent thief.
Still, she expects the stars will wear

five neat points, imagines the moon
with a fat nose, like the symbols
used even to this day on nursery walls.

> *Nikki, wake up.*
> *See the stars.*

Nikki struggles through muffling,
layered sleep. Her world of muted days
and cloud-reflected city glow at night
has
                  vanished. Overhead
the stars hang near,
intense and lapidary, as though
the gem-encrusted fabric of the sky
drooped with their weight.

Wondering, she lifts her hands. Sudden
hunger makes her fingers curl,
coveting glory, coveting their fire.
Stars suddenly as real
as the fizz of soda pop, as close
as sparklers on her birthday cake.

> *Will they be here tomorrow?*
> *No, just tonight.*
> *Aren't you a lucky girl*
> *to see the stars*
> *at least this once?*

But luck drains out of Nikki's eyes,
like starlight through her small,
plump fingers.

They won't be here
tomorrow?

The loss assaults her. Some birthright
snatched away before she knew
the heritage was hers. She is angry.
Her voice beats wings
above the reverent murmur of the crowd.

No! No!
I want them again
tomorrow.

The stars sing back to her, in
voices incandescent.

What if . . . a being from another planet were marooned on Earth?

THE STRANGER

Monica Hughes

Long before the time of the dinosaurs the Stranger had arrived. It saw them come and it saw them die out. Earth's continents drifted apart and, like a stony mass, it drifted with them. Marooned, light years from its home, it waited, lost in loneliness, as the first small mammals appeared. Millions of years passed, and still it waited . . . For food, certainly. But perhaps for something more.

The sun beat down upon the triangle of desert and the ancient rocks bore its heat silently. In the small shadow of a scattering of stones a turtle opened its yellow eyes to the sun and closed them again.

Beneath the surface the Stranger stirred restlessly. It gathered its powers and reached upwards, searching for – what *was* it searching for? Not food now, or it could have taken the turtle. Companionship perhaps? But there was nothing out there. The Stranger retreated to the cold loneliness at the center of its being and waited. Sometime. Sometime.

Roger sat opposite Dad and Dad's new wife, Susan, in the restaurant at the El Paso airport, and ate his way silently through an enchilada. Dad was trying to work out his flight plan on the chart in front of him, while Susan talked and talked. Since their marriage Roger had found himself longing for silence, a gift that had never seemed important to him before.

"It'll be so boring, Ted. Why don't I stay here with Roger until you finish working in Monterrey? You could pick us up on the way back."

Oh, no, Roger thought. The idea of being stuck alone with Susan filled him with horror and embarrassment.

Dad sighed patiently. "The whole point is to holiday in Mexico City after Monterrey. You'll love it there. Museums. Art galleries . . ."

Susan traced their route with her finger. "Then why don't you cut across country? We'd save a ton of time."

"It's safer flying by landmarks. Across the desert there's nothing."

"But it's so hot. So boring . . ."

Roger slipped on his Walkman headset and let music drown out their voices. He slurped his milkshake and then looked up to see his father's frown, his moving lips. He pulled off the headphones, "Huh?"

"You do it deliberately, don't you, Roger? Plugging in to that thing."

"My Walkman?"

"We're not stupid, you know. You're hurting Susan's feelings, cutting yourself off from us this way."

"It's just . . ." Roger hesitated and decided to go for the truth. "Well, I'm not crazy about listening to your fights, that's all."

Susan looked at her polished nails, dark red, matching her blouse. Dad muttered something about adjustments in any new family situation. Roger tuned out. He'd heard it all before.

"Time we were on our way," Dad said finally, and they went out into the white dusty heat. While Dad did the walkaround inspection Roger and Susan eyed each other as uneasily as two strange cats.

Dad taxied the rented Piper Seminole out and they waited in the broiling heat as a 737 took off. Then a DC3. In the seat next to Dad, Susan sighed and dabbed cologne on her forehead.

At last it was their turn and they trundled down the runway, picking up speed. Then there was the incredible high of take off, that feeling that all the weight of everyday life had been left behind on the ground. It got to Roger every time. Dad too. Roger could see the tension go out of his jaw.

He looked between Dad and Susan at the instrument panel. Just a few degrees off due south. The sky was a blue glass dish, clear from rim to rim. Beneath them the shadow of their plane crawled over the wrinkled brown earth. The highway between El Paso and Chihuahua was like a small thread, clueing them in.

Roger had picked up a guidebook in the airport, and now he sat back, riffling through the pages. A chapter title caught his eye. "The Zone of Silence." Just what this family needs, he thought. A zone of silence . . .

The desert area of Northern Mexico, at the junction of Chihuahua, Coahuila and Durango, harbors an electronic vortex that cuts out radio waves. There appears to be a magnetic field below the ground the force from which, rising in a funnel shape past Earth's atmosphere, also attracts meteorites and other objects flying over it.

Weird, thought Roger. More Susan's kind of thing than his. She was into UFOs and Atlantis and stuff like that. It drove Dad wild. Why had Dad married Susan? It seemed to Roger they had nothing in common. Why *her*?

"Roger, do you . . . do you miss your mother?" Dad had asked casually a while back.

Roger examined memories of tumbled brown hair and an infectious giggle. Of a game where he had hugged her and pretended that his arms wouldn't go around her waist. Memories of the smell of gingerbread and spicy meatloaf that were more real today than the photograph on his dressing table. "Sure I miss her."

It was then that Dad began talking about Susan. Roger had been quite pleased, thinking of decent meals instead of packaged this and microwaved that. And maybe someone to hug – not to replace Mom, he told himself quickly. Definitely not that. It was hard to put into words, even in his own mind – the thing that was missing in his life.

But when Dad brought her home for a pizza dinner Roger found out that Susan was small and blonde with a spectacular shape. And only eight years older than Roger, which he'd found out by sneaking a look at her driving license.

He'd been a numbly polite usher at their wedding and, after the honeymoon, he'd found himself avoiding both Susan and Dad as much as possible. *So what are we doing now, cooped up in a Piper Seminole over Northern Mexico?* he asked himself.

It had been Dad's harebrained scheme. Dad, desperate to make this new family work. "I have to go down to New Mexico for a consultation. Then a quick look at the new project in Monterrey. We can have a week's holiday in Mexico City. Get away from a Toronto winter. What could be better?"

Almost anything, thought Roger. And he knew Susan would rather have spent a week in Acapulco, sunning and drinking margaritas, not walking around museums and art galleries. Poor Dad, he just didn't see it.

The wings tipped. The ground and sky changed places and then went back to normal again. He glanced past Dad and Susan at the instrument panel. Dad had changed course, trying for the shortcut to Monterrey that Susan wanted. *I hope he knows what he's doing*, thought Roger. He looked down. No roads. No small green stains of irrigation. Only the wrinkled reddish brown of ancient land.

Beneath the rocks the Stranger stirred again. Had someone come at last in answer to its signal? Slowly it gathered its immense power from the cold sad core of its being and reached up, feeling, scanning, like the wavering pencil of a searchlight.

Roger could see Dad's lips move as he talked over the radio. He frowned, fiddling with the dial. Edgy. Roger could feel it.

"What's up?" He leaned forward, shouting in Dad's ear.

"Some sort of downdraft, though it doesn't make much sense so far from the mountains. And the radio's out."

According to the altimeter and the vertical speed indicator they were losing altitude, slowly but steadily.

"So pull her out of it, Dad," Roger shouted.

"I can't."

"Can't? Dad, it's the zone of silence. The guidebook said . . ."

"Not now, Rog."

"But it's this place. It attracts things and radio waves won't work."

"Like the Bermuda Triangle," Susan screamed and clutched Dad's arm. "Ted, we're going to crash."

"Not if we keep our heads. Susan, don't *do* that!"

"Listen, Dad! Change course. Bear west and get out of the vortex."

"What vortex? That's nonsense, Rog. There's nothing on God's green earth can pull a plane out of the sky."

"Then why are we losing altitude. What's going on?"

Dad ignored his questions. "Sit back and hold tight. I'm going to have to try a landing."

Roger gave up arguing. What was the point? The wrinkled land came closer. The wrinkles became the shadows on the east side of low ridges. Now he could see individual rocks. Now the ground was rushing beneath them. A long ridge loomed up, dead ahead. Roger shut his eyes, felt the plane lift, bounce, and come to a smooth stop.

He let out his breath and cautiously opened his eyes. Though Dad might be a real pain at times he could certainly handle a plane. He managed to keep his voice steady. "Nice work, Dad." He leaned forward to unlatch the door, pushed past Susan, and climbed down to the hot ground.

The landscape was as unreal and empty as Mars. Not even the shadow of a cloud moved across the land. The highest point seemed to be the ridge they had just cleared. Roger walked towards it, scrambled up the rocks, and looked around. The plane looked absurdly out of place, like a spread-winged albatross afloat on a sea of brown sand. Dad and Susan stood by the wing, two doll figures, arguing.

He turned his back on them. To the west and north the desert stretched to a saucer-rim horizon. The sun was over his left shoulder, pinning him to the ground like a beetle. There was no movement. *Nothing lives out here*, he thought. *Nothing at all.*

Come to me, begged the Stranger silently. *Come share my coldness, my loneliness. It has been so long since the last one . . .*

A small wind lifted a pillar of sand rose waist high off the ground and then collapsed. The sand scattered and was still.

Roger shivered. There was something spooky about this place. His mouth felt dry inside. He ran his tongue over his lips. They felt thick and cracked. He turned and ran down the ridge, back towards the plane, towards Dad and Susan.

"What did you see?"

"Nothing."

"What d'you mean, nothing?" Susan's voice was high. "There's got to be something."

Roger had no words for what he had seen and felt. He stretched out his arms, dropped them to his sides. "Nothing."

She began to cry. Dad put his arms round her. "It's all right, Susie-love. As soon as I've fixed the radio I can get a direction and set the autogyro. We've plenty of fuel. We'll be in Monterrey by sunset."

"Promise?"

"I promise. Sit in the shade. Relax. I won't be long."

His loving look made Roger turn his back and kick at the tires.

Dad swung up into the cabin. Roger could hear him whistling between his teeth. After a few minutes he climbed up to talk to him, "Dad, it's not going to work."

"Of course it is. Trust me."

"You weren't listening. You never listen to me now. The guidebook calls this place the Zone of Silence. It says . . ."

"Nonsense!"

"Have it your way then." Roger dropped to the ground. Susan was sitting in the shadow of the wing, twisting her fingers together.

"What did he say?" she asked.

"That he can fix it. But he can't. I told him before, but he wouldn't listen."

"Told him what?"

"This." He handed her the open guidebook and she began to read, her lips moving.

Roger's anger melted. He shouldn't have shown her the book. It'd only scare her. He tried to snatch it back, but she hunched away from him and went on reading. At the bottom of the page she stared up at him. "It's like I said. Like the Bermuda Triangle."

"Not really." He forced a laugh. "After all, we're not drowning."

They both stared at the swell of sand, the wrack of small withered cacti. Her lips trembled and she scrambled to her feet. "Ted. Ted!"

Roger caught her hand. It was warm and moist, the wrist as small as a child's. "It's just a dumb story."

She pulled her hand away and called again. Dad climbed onto the wing and jumped to the ground, easing his wet shirt from his back. "It's hot as Hades in that cabin. I'll have another try when it's cooler."

"What's the use? It's not going to work. It'll never work. We're trapped." Her voice rose.

"Nonsense. You're overreacting. You always . . ."

"I do not. Think about it, Ted. We don't have any food. Any water. We'll *die!*"

"They'll find us. As soon as they see we're overdue, they'll check our flight plan."

"But you changed it."

"You kept on at me."

"Didn't you notify them?"

"I was doing that when the radio went out."

"They'll never find us. Never."

Roger turned his back and put on his headset. The sun was dropping into the west and the shadow of the plane stretched eastward. He lay in it, his hands behind his head, shutting out their voices with music.

The sun set abruptly and the sky darkened. The stars shimmered in the heat rising from the desert. After a time they stopped shimmering and shone cold and clear. Roger shivered and climbed into the cabin for his sweater.

"What are you doing?" Dad's voice was shockingly loud in the silence. Roger told him. "Chuck down something for Susan, will you?"

He found a sweater Dad had bought for her, expensive alpaca, silky and warm. The feel of it in his hands made him wonder what it would be like to touch her hair. He dropped the sweater quickly at Dad's feet and walked away towards the ridge of rock.

Then the stars began to fall. Like the end of the world, he thought, and his heart lurched. But it was only a meteor shower. A real beauty. Cosmic fireworks. He lay on his back on top of the ridge and watched until he fell asleep.

Come, the Stranger begged, in a voice so deep Roger could not hear it, only feel it in his bones and in his dreaming. *Come, share my loneliness. Come.*

He woke to the sound of their voices, Susan accusing, Dad defending. Then she was hysterical and he soothing. *So, what's new?* Roger thought bitterly. *Oh, Mom, I do miss you. How could Dad . . .?* His eyes pricked with unexpected tears and he sat up, blinking, and plugged his ears with music.

The sun was still below the horizon and the air was cool. If there was any moisture in the air, there would be a dew. One could lick it off the rocks. He touched them. They were as dry as dinosaur bones.

Without asking himself what he was doing he began to walk north, away from Dad. From Susan. The ridge stretched into the distance like the backbone of some huge prehistoric creature.

Like a blood orange the sun popped up into the sky. Music filled his ears, shutting out the quarrels. Shutting out Susan. Shutting out both of them. When the tape ended he set it on replay and walked on blindly. He never heard the beat of helicopter blades coming out of the east, out of the sun, from Monterrey.

Come, said the Stranger. *Come, my friend.*

The wind blew. A pillar of sand whirled around Roger. When the wind dropped again the ridge was empty.

Welcome, said the Stranger.

What if ... only *you* can save the day but you don't know how?

ETERNITY LEAVE
Tim Wynne-Jones

When Camille Davidpieter died, I was the one who found her body.

In the papers it said, "The corpse of the world-famous writer was discovered by a young neighbor."

That's me, Amber Lightstone. The reporter even knows me. Molly O'Donnell writes for the local rag but her article about Camille's death was in all the big dailies. I mean, everywhere! That's because she sold the story to the wire service, her first international byline. I could have been a household name all over the world. People could have been reading about me while they ate their eggs and bacon or sticky rice or grasshoppers and gruel or whatever other people eat for breakfast. Instead, I was just "a young neighbor." She didn't even say what great friends Camille and I were. Nothing.

But it's not really Molly's fault. When one of the world's best loved science fiction writers dies, the person who finds the body isn't all that important in the scheme of things.

At least, that's the way it seemed, at first.

I had better tell you the whole story, so you'll understand why it ended up that I had to make sure Molly *didn't* mention my name. And I guess I'd better back up to the night *before* I found Camille's body. Because, like so many other things, the death of Camille Davidpieter was only an end in one sense of the word.

There was a harvest moon and, in the cornfields, the propane guns were firing at regular intervals to scare off the raccoons.

Boom, boom.

You get used to it, but that night I couldn't sleep. The night seemed to be whispering at me, "Amber Lightstone, there's huge stuff going on out here, and you're up there counting sheep." I got up and went to my window. There was a frog glommed to the window glass with his suction-cup feet. As I watched, his tongue darted out and snagged a moth.

Harvest time.

I opened my window, careful not to disturb the frog's midnight feast. Night noises scuttled into my room. Sleep-lessness was in the air. Owls and crickets and –

Boom, boom.

The guns were louder now, with the window open, more urgent sounding. The moon was so bright that the smoke from our chimney cast a snaky shadow across the driveway and into the grass. Then I heard a crunching sound that wasn't the frog. It was the sound gravel makes when it's not alone. A bicycle glided by the end of the driveway. A bicycle with flags. It was Beautiful Day.

Beautiful Day is what we kids call him. I don't think anybody knows his real name. He's forty or fifty and a real space cadet. All he ever says is, "Beautiful Day," even when it's pouring rain. Even if it's forty below.

"Hey, Beautiful Day," I wanted to yell at him, "It's the middle of the night." But yelling at someone in the middle of the night is almost as crazy as cycling down a country road in the middle of the night. So I kept the yell inside and my eyes peeled. He's harmless enough for a space cadet. But he didn't exactly look harmless bicycling past our house dragging a moon shadow behind him. What was he doing miles from town? Pedaling hard, that's what. A man with a mission.

It actually crossed my mind to follow him, but the idea never caught on with the rest of my body. I climbed back into bed, a little chilly, and lay there trying to imagine where he was going. What I ended up thinking about was where I would go if I were crazy enough to be out in the wee hours. The King's Head, that's where.

It's a rough hill rising up in the middle of the rolling corn fields near my place. It's a good name – I named it – because it looks just like a bearded king with a regal granite nose and craggy eyebrows. He's even got a crown, an old stone mill or silo or something open at the top. I stand in there sometimes and yell just to hear the echoes spiral up three, four stories to the sky. The King's Head is the highest point of land around; you can see for miles. I've been drawn there since I was little by a mysterious and irresistible force. That's what I told Camille once. Because she was a writer, she'd understand it when I said stuff like that. She was impressed.

Now, in my mind's eye, I stood on the King's Head and saw the landscape by moonlight. Sensational. If that's where Beautiful Day was heading, I was jealous of him. But not so jealous I was going to follow. What with the propane guns booming and the setting moon casting longer and longer shadows, the irresistible force wasn't anywhere near as irresistible as my bed.

Despite a restless night, I was up first thing. It was Saturday and my plan was to bicycle over to Camille's to see if she wanted anything from town. Camille lived at the end of the road in a little cottage, down in a valley by a stream. For a science fiction writer, the whole establishment was pretty low tech. There was no television, no computer.

"I write speculative fiction, Amber," she used to say. "And it's hard to speculate about what *might* come to pass if what *has* come to pass is buzzing and humming at you all the time."

"Yeah, but what about the Net?"

I remember her putting on a haughty face when I said that. "The net is what high-wire artists use when they are afraid they might fall."

Camille Davidpieter made up for her lack of electronic toys with a thousand gigabyte imagination. She believed imagination was the most powerful tool in the universe. I was only eight when I read her comic fantasy *Gray Matter* where this guy, Constantine Gray, figures out how to split the fairy-tale atom. But I've read her adult stuff, too, like *Entropy Means Nothing to Me*, and her last one, *Dustspeak*. It's about how everything is star dust because that is all there is, from the "tame dust bunnies under your bed to the swirling dust storm between your ears." Everything – the whole universe – is one long continuous unraveling and reraveling of star dust which we can only understand when our imagination resonates just right with the stardust. I used to think my imagination sort of resonated at the same frequency as Camille Davidpieter's, which is why we got along so well. But there were other reasons, reasons I didn't know about.

I had to pass by the King's Head on my way to Camille's. I was pumping hard up the road, but I had to glance over to see how the King was doing. He looked particularly grouchy that morning. Maybe, like me, the propane guns were getting on his nerves. Then I saw, lying by the side of the road, another bike. Beautiful Day's bike. I stopped. It was right by the bent old gate where a tractor trail led through the cornfield to the King's Head. And coming up the mucky trail was Beautiful Day, himself.

Boom, boom.

Beautiful Day jumped as if he had been shot. He saw me and jumped again. He stopped, afraid to come any closer.

"It's o-o-okay," I said. I stammer pretty badly. Can't help it. Camille used to say it's because I think too many thoughts at once. She also said I'd outgrow it. Anyway, I must have sounded a bit stunned and looked it, too. What was Beautiful Day up to out there that had got the King so mad? He edged towards me.

"Beau-beau-beautiful day," he said as if my stammer were catching. He looked pretty tired. And something else. Sad.

"D-d-didn't your sp-spa-spaceship c-c-c-come?" I said. I don't know why I said it. It was supposed to be a joke. But Beautiful Day's eyes got big and round and kind of hopeful as if he had finally found someone to share his secret with. He looked mournfully over his shoulder at the hill. Then he turned back to me and shook his head. He looked pretty disappointed, all right.

"Supposed to come," he said. "Full moon. Beautiful day."

Right. He *had* been waiting for a spaceship. I didn't know what to think, except that my little joke had put the idea in his head. I guess somebody had to put *something* in his head! Well, at least I could be a little help. There was something else I could cram in there along with the spaceship. If it was the full moon he was looking for, he was a day early.

"Th-the moo-ooOOn's f-f-full tonight," I said.

Beautiful Day's eyes lit up. He held up his arms and dropped them to his side as if that explained everything. "Thankee," he said, bowing to me. Then he tipped a hat he wasn't wearing and said, "Beautiful day."

I said, "Beautiful day" back and pushed on. Very strange. It would make for an interesting anecdote to tell Camille, I thought.

As I walked down her pathway, pushing my bike, I caught a glimpse of her at her writing desk. That was good news. She had been having trouble getting started on a new novel, but obviously she had overcome the problem. She never sat at her writing desk until she was ready to write.

"Sitting at a desk with nothing to write is balderdash!" she liked to say. "Do the dishes, weed the carrots. Make yourself useful. Only sit down to write when you have something to say."

I was glad she had something to say and I knew better than to disturb her. So I was about to turn and go when something made me stop. Something made me shiver. Something made me sneak a peek in her window.

Her silvery head was lying on her desktop. At first I thought she was just having a little nap. She was in her eighties, after all. She looked peaceful enough. Her fountain pen was still clutched in her hand.

I opened the door she never locked. "Miss D-D-Davidpieter?" No response. I went over and knelt beside her. "C-C-Camille?"

I touched her hand. Her skin was cold. The pen tumbled out of her grip leaving a smeary blob of shiny blue-black ink on her desk.

For some reason, I wasn't frightened. Not then. I wasn't even upset. Not yet. I was more curious than anything.

On her writing pad she had written a title and an opening
sentence:

> *Eternity Leave*
> Amber Lightstone had the kind of high octane
> imagination you need to fuel a starship.

I couldn't believe it. Me! I was going to be the protagonist
in her next novel. I was going to be a celebrity. I stood there
kind of dumb with shock, staring straight ahead. Above her
desk there was this lovely framed painting of a night sky
with a fanciful rocket ship, all glowy and thin as a Bunsen-
burner flame. I found myself staring at it and for a nano-
second the stars in the painted sky danced in my eyes. Then
it dawned on me: I wasn't going to be a celebrity. There
wasn't going to be a next novel. Because there wasn't any
Camille Davidpieter, anymore, to write it.

Suddenly, I started shuddering. I was frightened and angry
and heartbroken all at once. I couldn't stay in her cottage a
minute longer, not even to use her phone. I raced home,
passing Beautiful Day in a spray of gravel and tears without
so much as a word.

"Beautiful day," he yelled after me.

Mom called 911. Then she called Molly O'Donnell at her
home number.

"M-mom! Wh-wh-what if I'm wr-wr-wr-wrong?"

She frowned at me as if I'd better not be.

She told Molly the news, then handed me the phone.
Molly wanted to know all the details. "You must be sad," she
said. "I know you two were close." I didn't answer. I was too
busy wondering how she knew that.

"M-m-maybe I w-w-was wrong," I said. Mom frowned
again.

"I only wish you were," said Molly.

Which is why it came as a shock to everybody — myself, especially — when it turned out I was. Wrong, I mean.

Dead wrong.

It was about an hour later. I was in my room. I had cried a whole bunch more, put all Camille's books in chronological order, reread the inscriptions she had written to me, and cried again. Then Mom called me. She was standing at the bottom of the stairs.

"That was Molly," she said, wringing her hands. She looked a little gray around the gills. "It seems that she's alive, honey. Miss Davidpieter is alive!"

The weird thing was, Camille hadn't had a heart attack or a stroke. She hadn't even taken a nap! What's more, she hadn't been near her writing desk in days. That morning, she'd been out in her garden since dawn, which is where the ambulance attendants found her and where Molly found the ambulance attendants having a good old chat with the "deceased" about the benefit of growing marigolds near your beans.

Mom drove me over to apologize. Camille isn't a touchy-feely kind of person, but I almost hugged the life out of her. And wouldn't that have been disastrous! Dead twice on the same day! I felt like such an idiot.

The ambulance attendants had already left, but Camille had been good enough to explain that I wasn't the kind of girl who made crank calls. She also told them that she had been rather short of breath lately, and that, being a sensitive child, maybe I had dreamed the whole thing. I guess it was as much as I could hope for.

Molly kept looking at me oddly, which wasn't hard for Molly. She has bulgy eyes as if she'd been outfitted with extra large optic equipment in heaven, but they'd plum run out of large enough skulls. And to make matters spectacularly worse, her eyesight was lousy. She had to wear specs as thick as aquarium glass. Her eyes kind of swim around behind her glasses, like dolphins, or something. Friendly eyes. But that day, troubled. She looked like she'd had a pretty bad night herself and the last thing she needed was to be dragged out to the countryside on her day off for a hoax.

"I'm really sorry," I said to her. "I guess Miss Davidpieter is right."

Molly looked more quizzical than irritated. "Hey, don't sweat it," she said. "An active imagination is a powerful thing." She smiled kind of conspiratorially. I guess she read Camille's books, too. I smiled back. She waved at me as she drove off.

"I spent a good long time behind the scarlet runners, dear," said Camille to me later, when everyone else had gone. "Which is why I missed you, I suppose."

We were having tea in the garden. I had calmed down by then. Enough to know that her hanging out behind the scarlet runners didn't explain *anything*.

"It was s-s-so c-c-lear," I told her as I described what I had seen: the ink stain, the writing on the pad.

"You didn't by any chance catch what I had written, did you?" she asked.

I fibbed. I told her I was too upset to notice. Well, I didn't want her to think I had made the whole thing up just so that I could pretend I was the heroine of one of her stories.

"Well, I'm glad I was writing again," she said. She seemed to be pondering something, looking towards the wall of sunflowers that separated her garden from the meadow. The sunflowers were a pretty ragtag bunch that late in the season.

But they joined her in her meditation, a wise council of tired old yellow-faced friends. I kept perfectly still.

After a while she looked at me gravely. "Tell me about last night," she said.

It was like a thunderbolt. What did last night have to do with anything? Unless, of course, she thought it was all just a dream. But I told her. About not being able to sleep, about seeing Beautiful Day bicycle by.

"Beautiful Day?" She had never heard him called that – she didn't get into town much. Still, she knew who I meant, right away. She seemed particularly interested. So I went on to tell her about running into him again at the King's Head on my way over.

She raised an eyebrow. "Go on."

"I asked h-h-h-h-him if h-his sp-sp-spaceship had c-c-c-come," I said. "The one b-b-bringing him a b-b-brain."

Camille smiled at me, but it wasn't one of those patronizing aren't-you-a-naughty-girl smiles. It was actually a little scary.

"What made you say that?" she asked.

I tried to think. What makes me say anything? I shrugged. "It just c-c-c-came to me," was all I could say.

She nodded and her smile brightened to three hundred watts as if that was the very answer she had been hoping for.

"Wh-what's g-g-going on, Camille?" I asked, uneasily.

She looked at me, looked out at the sunflowers nodding in the afternoon breeze. The sunflowers seemed to give her the okay.

"I always rather expected this of you, Amber," she said. "You're beginning to know beyond knowing."

I was about to blush and thank her when the gist of what she was saying hit me like a meteorite. "No!" I said. "You're n-n-n-n-not g-g-going to die!"

She gave me a look as if to say, "Oh, come now, dear." Mercifully she didn't say it, or I'd have been really angry. I hate being treated like a kid. Instead, she waited until I had come to grips with the idea, myself.

Of course, she was going to die, sometime. Everyone does. And if she was saying that I had foreseen the circumstances of her death it didn't necessarily mean it was going to happen soon. All the same, I wasn't happy with the news. And I wasn't convinced — even coming from her. Having a brain so full of junk I couldn't talk straight was one thing; seeing things that were actually going to take place was something else. But there wasn't much time to think about this newfound talent before she hit me with another bombshell.

"Beautiful Day, as you call him — he also has this gift."

Beautiful Day, gifted! I felt suddenly light-headed, my body boneless. I felt as if all I had inside me was space. I had to grip the arms of the wicker garden chair to stop from slipping right out of it into a little Amber puddle on the patio steps.

Camille apologized and fussed over me, making me sip sweet tea and eat a biscuit, as she calls them, and generally, not fade away on her right yet.

"Perhaps I should have told you earlier," she said. "But, you see, I had to wait for a sign. A real sign."

Camille, by then, was hurrying me inside. She had decided that the sun was responsible for my light-headedness — it was awfully bright for October. She led me, a little dazed, into the coolth of the kitchen. I don't know if there is such a word as coolth but, coming in out of the buzzing warmth, that's how it felt.

As soon as she sat down and our eyes met, I got another

jolt, and I didn't like it. I knew beyond knowing exactly what she was going to say next.

"And y-y-y-you," I said. "You h-h-h-have visions – the g-g-gift. You have i-i-i-it, too." It wasn't a question and so she didn't bother to answer me.

A few minutes earlier, I had felt totally empty. Now, that endless space in me seemed to be filling up, very quickly, with a whole swirling mass of passing stardust. I knew, somehow, that I was a chosen one. I mean that Camille had chosen me. I knew that she had been preparing me. That it was almost time. That running into Beautiful Day wasn't a coincidence. He was in on it, too, somehow. Something was happening or was going to happen soon. But there were some things I didn't know. Little things like: Why? When? What? How? or How Much?

"Like you and Beautiful Day," she said. "I couldn't sleep a wink last night. My thoughts turned to the King's Head. Like you, I did not venture to go there. I am too old, now, for clambering around in the dark. Besides, I was not needed. Not this time. And you, Amber, you are too young; your time is still to come. Each of the chosen ones is called at his or her appointed time. It is Beautiful Day's turn, which has worried me – what, with his condition and all. But bless his muddled head – he was there. He made it. Well, a day early. But that's fine. Kind of a dress rehearsal."

"A d-d-dress reheeeeearsal for wh-wh-what?"

Camille clammed up, a pained look on her face. She put one of her soft wrinkly hands on mine. "I mustn't say."

"Why-wh-why not?" I demanded.

She closed her eyes. How tired she looked. I hated bugging her, but I hated the feelings that were smashing around in me like loose electrons looking for a fight.

"It's what I've told you about your writing, Amber. You know, show don't tell."

She had said it enough times, all right. I knew what she meant. Always paint a picture, if you can, instead of explaining. "O-k-k-kay," I said. I leaned back in my chair, back straight, alert, expecting her to paint a picture for me.

She only shook her head. "I'm afraid the show isn't until tonight."

I groaned. It wasn't like her to act so secretively.

"You must understand," she said. "I can't tell you what it is you are going to see. Only after you have seen it, will we be sure you are one of us." She looked quite worried for a moment. The look on her face said: *What if I've made a mistake about Amber?* I didn't feel ready to be depended upon. I felt all used up. And yet I wanted desperately to be a we — whoever we were — and not just an I.

Her frown vanished. She sensed my frustration. "You mustn't fret, Amber," she said. "All the signs suggest you are perfectly ready."

I moped. Camille didn't have much time for mopers, but it was better than the alternative which was to blow my top.

"I d-d-d-don't like m-m-mysteries!"

To my surprise, she chuckled, which only made me madder. I get laughed at a fair bit by kids because of my speech impediment. I hate being laughed at — who doesn't? — even more than I hate mysteries. But Camille wasn't laughing at me; I knew that. She raised her hand in peace.

"Don't you remember?" she said. "That was the first thing you said to me when I came to speak at your school. 'I don't like mysteries,' you said. And then you told me that you did like science fiction because it wasn't about hiding things but about discovering things."

"I s-s-said that?"

She nodded. "Indeed you did. And it was a very clever thing to say. I've often quoted you." Then she leaned forward and warmly took my hand in hers. "And shortly, you are going to discover something quite marvelous, Amber."

"It c-c-c-c-can't be sh-sh-SHort enough!" I grumbled. Then I hung my head. Tantrums are a real drag when you stutter.

Camille didn't say anything. When I glanced up she was looking at me, kindly. "You wouldn't thank me for giving away the ending."

Her tone of voice was firm. She didn't want any more questions, let alone tantrums. And the truth is, I was kind of tantrummed out. But, oh, I was nervous. Like those dreams where you're just about to go on stage and you don't know your lines. Except, in this case, I didn't even know what play I was in! "Wh-wh-what do I h-h-h-have to do?" I asked.

"What you have to do," she said, very precisely, "is only what you did when you saw Beautiful Day this morning."

"Namely?"

She twinkled at me. I hate it when adults twinkle at you. And what she said didn't help matters. She said, "Whatever comes to mind."

I rolled my eyes. What kind of advice was that? But when I looked at her, her eyes seemed to say to me: *You know all you need to know for now. Be still.*

I sighed and beed still.

"Good girl," she said. And then she got a look on her face as if she was going through a mental checklist to make sure I really did know all I needed to know. I waited apprehensively.

"A chosen one – and there are others – is never called upon until ready. I took a long time myself.

"I was a very troubled child. What they call autistic, now-adays. I never spoke. Never. But with the help of a wonderful teacher I discovered painting. With paint it seemed I could say all the things for which I had no words. I was quite talented and people made a fuss over me. That's how Solly Marvel found out about me."

This made my ears prick up. I knew Solomon Marvel – as a library!

"The very same," she said. "The Potter's Hat Library was named after him. He was a wonderful man. And when he saw what I was painting, he knew I was one of the chosen. He knew I would need to be prepared, in much the way I have tried to prepare you.

"My time did not come until I was twenty-two, Amber. Oh, how frustrating it was. And how frustrating Solly was. He wouldn't tell me any particulars, but, somehow, he was able to convince me that I was special."

Special how? She wasn't saying. More mystery. More wait and see. I crossed my arms and gritted my teeth and gave Camille one of my patented glares of protest. She beamed it right back at me. That was all I was going to get out of her, right then. Come to think of it, the way she beamed at me was pretty special.

The harvest moon was finally set, the night charged with energy, all the stars on fire. If I had never met Camille Davidpieter, if that day had just been a totally ordinary fall day, I still would have had a hard time sleeping. I had gone to bed fully dressed, not knowing what to expect, only that I was to expect something. I left my window open wide. I left my mind open wide. Sometime after two, a bicycle passed my driveway and I was up in a shot.

Boom, boom.

I stood on my front doorstep bathed in moonlight, my bike helmet in my hand. It was a cool night, frost was in the air, but my bed was a long way behind me. If I had never met Beautiful Day, if I had never run into him over at the King's Head, I still would have known where I had to go.

Boom, boom.

I stayed far behind him, not wanting to frighten him, to throw him off.

Your time is still to come. It's Beautiful Day's turn.

By the time I leaned my bike up against the fence post at the tractor trail, he was already up at the Head. I could just make him out standing by the King's crown, his head tilted upwards scanning the sky. His scraggly hair was blowing. There was a breeze up there. Cold.

Boom, boom.

I tried to time the automatic blasts of the propane guns so that they didn't scare me out of my wits every time they went off. It didn't work. The anticipation only made matters worse.

I made my way towards the hill, keeping close to the towering wall of cornstalks rustling in the breeze. I didn't want Beautiful Day to see me. I don't know if I was more afraid for him or of him. I had once joked about being drawn to the King's Head by an irresistible force. It wasn't a joke. It was drawing me now and it had already drawn Beautiful Day. Maybe it drew all the loonies. I stopped and looked around, suddenly afraid that there may be others of us there, a whole army of space cadets. The cornstalks cast shadows of skeletons dancing.

Boom, boom.

The ground had been churned up by tractor wheels; it was mucky. I stepped right out of my sneaker once. I had to stand on one foot and bend down to lift it out of the guck. That's when I came face-to-face with six beady eyes staring at me. I swallowed a scream. You don't expect aliens to be knee-high.

Then the eyes scuttled off and I let out my breath. You don't expect aliens to be raccoons, either.

But my relief was short-lived. The next sound I heard was not the propane guns. It was not anything so harsh or mechanical sounding. I looked up. I didn't see anything – not at first. But the sound was definitely coming from above. It was like the sound the stars might make if you could find the on button. It was like singing. It was drawing nearer. I stepped away from the wall of corn.

It's a cloud, I thought. A cloud with very tidy sides. A cloud that is unnaturally bright and stalled in the air while beyond it other ragged, ordinary-looking darker clouds were scudding along before a stiff breeze. I took a full long look before I abandoned the cloud idea and gave in to what my senses had told me from the beginning. I was looking at a starship hovering high above the field.

It was long and slim and dimly silvery as if the moonlight had fused it into a cylinder. No fins. No rings. As sleek and tapered as a torch flame.

I looked towards the King's Head; Beautiful Day saw it, too. He was jumping up and down and waving and singing along with the ship. He was even singing in the same key.

Now, from all around me, there was a wild disturbance as a field full of fearless corn thieves suddenly fled for their lives, screeching as the singing ship above them slowly descended.

Beautiful Day was speaking to the ship, yelling through cupped hands, waving it on in. He pointed towards the silo-like structure and nodded his head as if he and the ship had come to some kind of an understanding. He slapped the side of the tower. He started laughing like a maniac. He twirled around and around.

I looked up again and the needle-like ship began to rotate slowly counterclockwise until its tapered nose was at midnight and its tail was at six o'clock. Then it moved until it was directly above the silo. It was going to land.

The silo was some kind of landing bay!

Then I heard an agonizing cry from the hill and was just in time to see Beautiful Day dance himself right off the side of the King's Head.

An awful roar went up from the ship. It sounded like someone had let a mouse loose in a massed choir. It was a kind of screaming and indecipherable chattering. There were no words to it – just raw fear. Raw, ear-shattering fear. There was only one reason for it I could think of. Beautiful Day. The ship needed him. I had to help. It wasn't my time – that's what Camille had said – but I had to do what I could. We were in this together, weren't we?

I raced towards the hill, then crashed through the corn rows that covered the King's left shoulder. I kept glancing at the ship hovering in suspended animation above the silo. Was it my imagination, or was it beginning to fade?

I heard a cry up ahead. It was Beautiful Day. He was lying in a heap, half buried in a gravel slide. His leg was bent in an odd way. Broken.

"Beautiful day," he said.

"N-n-n-no it's n-n-not!" I said. "It's the middle of th-the f-f-freaking night. A-a-and there's this sp-p-p-paceshhhhip!"

He was looking at it; I could see it reflected in his eyes. That was all I could see in his eyes. He was totally out of it. He started pounding his fists on the ground.

They sure needed something. The sound from the ship had become unbearable. But when I looked up, to my shock, the ship had faded still further. It was almost transparent.

I shook Beautiful Day. He cried out in agony. I got to my knees and made him look into my eyes.

"Wh-wh-what can I d-d-d-d-do?" I asked.

He looked from me to the spaceship and started trying to get to his feet. Apparently, climbing the hill on a broken leg was easier than trying to explain to me what had to be done. He winced with pain and crumpled to the ground. Then his eyes filled with a kind of horrified hope.

"Inside!" he said, grabbing my arm. He jabbed his finger towards the hill, the silo, the ship – I didn't know what.

"Inside wh-wh-wh-where?"

"The crown," he said.

It wasn't much to go on.

I scrambled up the King's rugged cheek, cutting myself on his brambly hair, finding footholds in his pitted skin. Above me the sound of the ship was shrill but diminishing in volume. It was as if it was using all its remaining energy to call for help. And it seemed I was its last hope.

But what? What could I do?

I made the hilltop and dashed across the uneven ground to the doorway in the silo's side. The door was long since gone. I stepped inside, looked up, and ducked. The ship's tail perfectly filled the mouth of the silo. What light the ship still emitted washed the gray stone walls.

What now?

Whatever comes to you.

I looked up again. The song of the ship was rapidly diminishing, little more than a massed moan now. I began to be able to hear myself think. And this is what I thought:

Walk out there, Amber, to the middle of the silo, to the place where you sometimes yell just to hear the echo. Stand there, Amber. It will be enough.

"I c-c-c-can't," I told myself. But myself wasn't listening.

You can do anything you can imagine, my thoughts answered back. My thoughts sounded very confident. They spoke with Camille's voice.

I looked up again. The ship looked like a ghost ship. I could see the night sky through it. It was dying. It was now or never. I took a deep breath and walked out to the center of the silo. Immediately, the ship started to descend.

"I'm going to be crushed," I thought, squeezing my eyes tightly shut. "This is my destiny: to be a landing pad for a four-story-high intergalactic starship."

I clenched my fists. I dared to squint upwards through one eye. It was almost on top of me. What was I doing!

What comes to you.

There was no escape, anyway. Even if I ran I'd never make it to the doorway in time. My head sunk into my shoulders. I raised my hands above my head, prepared for contact.

I guess there was a moment where I knew it had touched me, landed – landed on me. My knees buckled, but only out of reflex. The thing coming down on me was weightless. In another instant it was passing right through me, or I was passing through it, I couldn't say. But when I dared to open my eyes again it was all around me, engulfing me. I was inside.

Instantaneously, I felt my mind emptying. It didn't hurt. I wasn't about to faint or anything. Not only that, it felt kind of good! And it seemed to be doing some good, for the light-ship was growing in intensity. I looked around me. There were no walls, no floors, no furniture – just light in every shade of color. Gleaming and streaming. As I watched, some of the light thickened into amorphous shapes. Beings of some kind. The shapes had nothing you could really call eyes, but I knew they were happy to see me. They had nothing you could really identify as mouths either, but they were singing again. Not shrieking now. A soothing sound.

The beings *were* the ship: the ship *was* the beings. And they were feeding off me. It was my imagination they wanted. I gave it willingly and the thing around me grew brighter, stronger. The miraculous thing was that I didn't feel any weaker. It did not drain me, I just felt clearer as if a weight was being lifted from me. It was as if I had been saving up for this for years.

I don't know how long I stood there. Long enough for the ship's light to become too bright to look at anymore. I closed my eyes, swaying a bit to the music without fear of falling. I was held up by light. Then, at last, I could feel it leaving me, feel it rising. I let it go. You cannot hold onto imagination.

When I opened my eyes again, I was just in time to see the recharged ship clear the mouth of the silo and shoot straight up into the moonbright sky, a brilliant flash like a shooting star. But not a shooting star burning up in the earth's gravity. A shooting star given the life to go on – to who knows where.

The refueling used up most of the night. Dawn was coming. Another day. The sounds of the world came to me. Owls and crickets and . . .

Boom, boom.

I don't know how he managed it, but when I looked towards the door, Beautiful Day was silhouetted there. He was leaning in the doorway staring at me.

"You okay?" I asked, coming towards him.

He sniffed and scratched his head, looking at me funny. He smiled, sheepishly. He shifted his weight and buckled over with pain. I helped him sit down with his back against the wall outside, facing east where the sun would rise sometime in the next hour or so.

"Nice girl," he said, pointing down the hill. "Helped me when I fell."

"That was me," I said. It was too much for him. He threw his head back and looked at the spot in the sky where the ship had gone. "They comin' from forever," he said. "Tha's what Miss D. telled me. They comin' from the heart of forever."

I wasn't sure where the heart of forever might be, but I figured it had to be at least a suburb of Eternity.

"They comed here, once upon a time. Brought life here. Now they stop here on their way to other places."

"To refuel," I said.

Beautiful Day nodded. Then he looked sadly down at his leg. I would have to get help for him, soon. But it wasn't his leg he was really thinking about.

"I wish I done it right," he said. He sounded so forlorn.

I patted him on the shoulder. "Next time," I said. He tried to cope with that. "I'll help you." He looked like he was going to thank me, but he'd run clear out of words. His eyes kind of glazed over. He had said about as much as he was going to. Well, almost. He looked at me one more time with something like the gaze of an intelligent life-form.

"Your stutter's gone," he said.

He was right. He knew it and smiled with satisfaction.

"Beautiful day," he said.

He was right about that, too.

I got help for Beautiful Day from the nearest farmer and went home for some breakfast. No one was up; no one knew I'd been gone. I changed. My bed called out to me, but I resisted the temptation. I felt oddly charged up. So what if I had been up all night; I could be good and tired later. Right now, there was somewhere I had to go.

Well, you know where, and I've already told you what I found when I got there.

Camille Davidpieter slumped over her writing desk, dead.

I stood for a long time stroking her soft old hair. I didn't know what else to do. Somehow, this time I knew it wasn't a vision, but the real thing. She was really gone.

Eternity Leave. What did it mean? That the beings on the ship were leaving eternity behind? Or maybe that they were carrying it everywhere – distributing it to habitable planets throughout the universe? Camille would have made that clear in her book. Now, it would never be written.

But as I stood there, I wondered if Camille had really been starting a new book, or whether, knowing she was dying, she had written a last message for my eyes only. To let me know what was in store for me.

Carefully, so as not to disturb her, I tore off the top page of her writing pad, folded it, and put it in my pocket. It would be our secret. There was no way I could ever let anyone know about this. Even if there were anyone who'd believe me.

At that moment I felt lonelier than I had ever felt in my life.

Then I heard a car arriving. I froze. I heard a car door slam. I couldn't move. There was someone on the path, someone opening the door without knocking.

It was Molly.

She stopped in her tracks when she saw me, but she didn't look all that surprised. She looked at me and then at Camille. Her face tightened in sorrow. Then I saw her boots; they were covered in muck.

She closed the door behind her. She raked her fingers through her tangly hair. There was something trapped there. A pale dry corn husk. She smiled at the look of surprise on my face. It was a warm sad smile.

"You did a good job, Amber," she said. "We knew you would."

Wh∂t if . . . something still lurks in the culvert?

THE TUNNEL

Sarah Ellis

When I was a kid and imagined myself older, with a summer job, I thought about being outdoors. Tree planting, maybe. Camping out, getting away from the parents, coming home after two months with biceps of iron and bags of money. I used to imagine myself rappelling down some mountain with a geological hammer tucked into my belt. At the very worst I saw myself sitting on one of those tall lifeguard chairs with zinc ointment on my lips.

I didn't know that by the time I was sixteen it would be the global economy and there would be no summer jobs, even though you did your life-skills analysis as recommended by the guidance counselor at school. Motivated! Energetic! Computer-literate! Shows initiative! Workplace-appropriate hair! What I never imagined was that by the time I got to be sixteen, the only job you could get would be babysitting.

I sometimes take care of my cousin, Laurence. Laurence likes impersonating trucks and being held upside down. I am good at assisting during these activities. This evidently counts as work-related experience.

Girls are different.

Elizabeth, who calls herself Ib, is six and one-quarter years old. I go over to her place at 7:30 in the morning and I finish at one o'clock. Then her dad or her mom or her gran (who is not really her gran but the mother of her dad's ex-wife) takes over. Ib has a complicated family. She doesn't seem to mind.

Ib has a yellow plastic suitcase. In the suitcase are Barbies. Ib would like to play with Barbies for five and one-half hours every day. In my babysitting course at the community center they taught us about first aid, diapering, nutritious snacks, and how to jump your jollies out. They did not teach Barbies.

"You be Wanda," says Ib, handing me a nude Barbie who looks as though she is having a bad hair day.

I'm quite prepared to be Wanda if that's what the job requires. But once I *am* Wanda, I don't know what the heck to do.

Ib is busy dressing Francine, Laurice, Betty, and Talking Doll, who is not a Barbie at all, but a baby doll twice the size of the Barbies.

"What should I do?" I ask.

Ib gives me The Look — an unblinking stare that combines impatience, scorn, and pity. "*Play*," she says.

When you have sixteen-year-old guy hands, there is no way to hold a nude Barbie without violating her personal space. But all her clothes seem to be made of extremely form-fitting stretchy neon stuff, and I can't get her rigid arms with their poky fingers into the sleeves.

Playing with Barbies makes all other activities look good. The study of irregular French verbs, for example, starts to seem attractive. The board game Candyland, a favorite of Laurence and previously condemned by me as a sure method of turning the human brain into tofu, starts to seem like a laff-riot.

I look at my watch. It is 8:15. The morning stretches ahead of me. Six weeks stretch ahead of me. My life stretches ahead of me. My brain is edging dangerously close to the idea of eternity.

I hold Wanda by her hard, claw-like plastic hand and think of things that Laurence likes to do. We could notch the edge of yogurt lids to make deadly star-shaped tonki for a Ninja attack, but somehow I don't think that's going to cut it with Ib. She's probably not going to go for a burping contest, either.

A warm breeze blows in the window – a small wind that probably originated at sea and blew across the beach, across all those glistening, slowly browning bodies, before it ended up here, trapped in Barbie World. I'm hallucinating the smell of suntan oil. I need to get outside.

I do not suggest a walk. I know, from Laurence, that "walk" is a four-letter word to six-year-olds. Six-year-olds can run around for seventy-two hours straight, but half a block of walking and they suffer from life-threatening exhaustion. I therefore avoid the W-word.

"Ib, would you like to go on an exploration mission?"

Ib thinks for a moment. "Yes."

We pack up the Barbies.

"It's quite a long walk," I say. "We can't take the suitcase."

"I need to take Wanda."

We take Wanda. We walk along the overgrown railway tracks out to the edge of town. Ib steps on every tie. The sun is behind us and we stop every so often to make our shadows into letters of the alphabet.

("And what sort of work experience can you bring to this job, young man?"

"Well, sir, I spent one summer playing with Barbie dolls and practicing making my body into a K."

"Excellent! We've got exciting openings in that area.")

We follow the tracks as the sun rises high in the sky. Ib walks along the rail holding my hand. My feet crunch on the sharp gravel and Ib sings something about chicks. I inhale the dusty smell of sunbaked weeds, and I'm pulled back to the summer when we used to come out here, Jeff and Danielle and I. That was the summer that Jeff was a double agent planning to blow up the enemy supply train.

The sharp sound of a pneumatic drill rips through the air, and Ib's hand tightens in mine.

"What's that?"

I remember. "It's just a woodpecker."

There was a woodpecker back then, too.

"Machine gun attack!" yelled Jeff. And I forgot it was a game and threw myself down the bank into the bushes. Jeff laughed at me.

"No lit-tle ducks came swim-ming back." Ib's high thin voice is burrowing itself into my brain, and there is a pulse above my left eye. I begin to wish I had brought something to drink. Maybe it's time to go back.

And then we come to the stream. I hear it before I see it. And then I remember what happened there.

Ib jumps off the track and dances off towards the water.

I don't want to go there. "Not that way, Ib."

"Come *on*, Ken. I'm exploring. This is an exploration mission. You said."

I follow her. It's different. The trees – dusty, scruffy-looking cottonwoods – have grown up, and the road appears too soon. But there it is. The stream takes a bend and disappears into a small culvert under the road. Vines grow across the entrance to the drainage pipe. I push them aside and look in. A black hole with a perfect circle of light at the end.

It's so small. Had we really walked through it? Jeff and Danielle and finally me, terrified, shamed into it by a girl and a double-dare.

I take a deep breath and I'm there again. That smell. Wet and green and dangerous.

There I was, feet braced against the pipe, halfway through the tunnel at the darkest part. I kept my mind up, up out of the water where Jeff said blackwater bloodsuckers lived. I kept my mind up until it went right into the weight of the earth above me. Tons of dirt and cars and trucks and being buried alive.

Dirt pressing heavy against my chest, against my eyelids, against my legs which wouldn't move. Above the roaring in my ears, I heard a high snatch of song. Two notes with no words. Calling. I pushed against the concrete and screamed without a sound.

And then Jeff yelled into the tunnel, "What's the matter, Kenny? Is it the bloodsuckers? Kenton, Kenton, where are you? Ve vant to suck your blood." Jeff had a way of saying "Kenton" that made it sound like an even finkier name than it is.

By this time I had peed my pants, and I had to pretend to slip and fall into the water to cover up. The shock of the cold. The end of the tunnel. Jeff pushed me into the stream because I was wet already. Danielle stared at me and she knew.

"Where does it go?" Ib pulls on my shirt.

I'm big again. Huge. Like Talking Doll.

"It goes under the road. I walked through it once."

"Did you go to that other place?"

"What other place?"

Ib gives me The Look. "Where those other girls play. I think this goes there."

Yeah, right. The Barbies visit the culvert.

Ib steps right into the tunnel. "Come on, Kenton."

I grab her. "Hey! Hold it. You can't go in there. You'll . . . you'll get your sandals wet. And I can't come. I don't fit."

Ib sits down on the gravel and takes off her sandals. "I fit."

Blackwater bloodsuckers. But why would I want to scare her? And hey, it's just a tunnel. So I happen to suffer from claustrophobia. That's my problem.

"Okay, but look, I'll wait on this side until you're halfway through and then I'll cross the road and meet you on the other side. Are you sure you're not scared?"

Ib steps into the pipe and stretches to become an X. "Look! Look how I fit!"

I watch the little X splash its way into the darkness.

"Okay, Ib, see you on the other side. Last one there's a rotten egg." I let the curtain of vines fall across the opening.

I pick up the sandals and climb the hill. It's different, too. It used to be just feathery horsetail and now skinny trees grow there. I grab onto them to pull myself up. I cross the road, hovering on the center line as an RV rumbles by, and then I slide down the other side, following a small avalanche of pebbles. I kneel on the top of the pipe and stick my head in, upside down.

"Hey, rotten egg, I beat you."

Small, echoing, dripping sounds are the only answer.

I peer into the darkness. She's teasing me.

"Ib!"

Ib, Ib, Ib – the tunnel throws my voice back at me. A semi-trailer roars by on the road. I jump down and stand at the pipe's entrance. My eyes adjust and I can see the dim green O at the other end. No outline of a little girl.

A tight heaviness grips me around the chest.

"Ibbie. Answer me right now. I mean it." I drop the sandals.

She must have turned and hidden on the other side, just to fool me.

I don't remember getting up the hill and across the road, except that the noise of a car horn rips across the top of my brain.

She isn't there. Empty tunnel.

"Elizabeth!"

She slipped. She knocked her head. Child drowns in four inches of bath water.

I have to go in. I try walking doubled over. But my feet just slip down the slimy curved concrete and I can only shuffle. I drop to my hands and knees.

Crawl, crawl, crawl, crawl.

The sound of splashing fills my head.

Come back, Elizabeth.

Do not push out against the concrete. Just go forward, *splash, splash.*

Do not think up or down.

Something floats against my hand. I gasp and jerk upwards, cracking my head. It's Wanda. I push her into my shirt. My knee bashes into a rock, and there is some sobbing in the echoing tunnel. It is my own voice.

And then I grab the rough ends of the pipe and pull myself into the light and the bigness.

Ib is crouched at the edge of the stream pushing a floating leaf with a stick. A green light makes its way through the trees above.

She looks at me and sees Wanda poking out of my shirt. "Oh, good, you found her. Bad Wanda, running away."

My relief explodes into anger.

"Ib, where were you?"

"Playing with the girls."

"No, quit pretending. I'm not playing. Where were you when I called you from this end of the tunnel? Were you hiding? Didn't you hear me call?"

"Sure I heard you, silly. That's how they knew my name. And I was going to come back but it was my turn. They never let me play before but this time they knew my name and I got to go into the circle. They were dancing. Like ballerinas. Except they had long hair. I get to have long hair when I'm in grade two."

My head is buzzing. I must have hit it harder than I realized. I hand Wanda to Ib and grab at some sense.

"Why didn't you come when I called you?"

"They said I wasn't allowed to go, not while I was in the circle, and they were going to give me some cake. I saw it. It had sprinkles on it. And then you called me again but you said 'Elizabeth.' And then they made me go away."

Ib blows her leaf boat across the stream. And then she starts to sing.

> "Idey, Idey, what's your name,
> What's your name to get in the game?"

The final puzzle piece of memory slides into place.

That song, the two-note song. The sweet high voice calling me in the tunnel. The sound just before Jeff called me back by my real name.

They wanted me. They wanted Ib. I begin to shiver.

I find myself sitting on the gravel. The stream splashes its way over the lip of the pipe into the tunnel. I stare at Ib, who looks so small and solid. My wet jeans with their slime-green knees begin to steam in the sun. A crow tells us a thing or two.

"Ken?"

"Yes?"

"I don't really like those girls."

"No, they don't sound that nice. Do you want to go home?"

"Okay."

I rinse off my hands and glance once more into the darkness.

"Put on your sandals, then."

Ib holds onto the back belt loops of my jeans, and I pull her up the hill, into the sunshine.

Wh⅃t if . . . the moon were haunted?

MOON MAIDEN
Alison Baird

"You can't do it, sis," Matt had said. And he had looked down his nose at her in his maddening, superior way. Matt was no giant himself, but it was easy to look down at Kate.

"Oh, yeah?" She'd glared up at her brother, hands on hips. "Well, I don't care what you think, I'm going. What's the point of winning a lunar study scholarship if you don't use it?"

It had been a hot and smoggy day, she remembered, with an ultraviolet alert, so the two of them had been stuck indoors and Matt, as usual, had taken out his boredom and frustration on Kate.

"One: you're way too young —"

"I'm nearly fourteen!"

"Two: you're a nitwit," Matt had finished.

And that settled it. After that "nitwit," no power in the universe could have prevented Kate Iwasaki from embarking on the shuttle for Luna Base.

But Matt had had a parting shot. "You'll never spend half a year on the Moon! You'll end up going crazy, like all those loony Lunies."

Kate had shivered at that; she'd heard about the moon-madness. It started with hallucinations. Then you began talking to imaginary people, even yelling and screaming at them, or sometimes recoiling from invisible horrors. That was when the security guards came and "escorted" you away. It was a fact of life on Luna Base; some people just could not take the claustrophobic atmosphere: the isolation was worse than on the most remote polar weather station or deep-sea lab on Earth.

But Kate firmly pushed her fears aside. She was too sensible, too *scientific*, to ever lose control like that – or so she told herself. "I'm going, and that's that," she had declared, lifting her chin.

Now she smiled with satisfaction as the small lunar shuttle carrying her and the other students planed low over the surface of the Mare Tranquillitatis. Through the window she could see flat plains of ash-colored lunar soil – *regolith*, the instructor called it – strewn with modest-sized impact craters, some no more than a decimeter across. *Not too impressive*, Kate thought. She'd already been on much more spectacular trips, to the giant craters Tycho and Copernicus, and to the lunar mountain ranges, the Alps and Apennines. But this outing was always the most popular. The shuttle's interior was crammed to capacity with eager students.

The spacecraft slowed and hovered briefly before setting down gently on its four wide landing pods. The cabin ceased to thrum and vibrate as the engines were cut, and a flashing light came on over each air lock. The students all rose and shuffled down the aisle in their cumbersome space suits, pulling on their helmets.

"All right, to the air locks, just four at a time now," the instructor told them as he checked their helmet seals. "And don't stampede; form proper lines."

Kate managed to be one of the first in the air locks. She held her breath as the metal door slid open, and all sound ceased with the release of the air. When they climbed out, most of the kids bounced around like demented kangaroos the minute they reached the surface. Kate just stood looking up at the sunlit face of Earth, its blue-white glow fifty times brighter than the brightest moonlight. Poor polluted overcrowded Earth! No, she wasn't in any great hurry to go back there.

With some difficulty the instructor managed to herd them all together and direct them to their destination. At the sight of it, the students began to babble with excitement.

Tranquillity Base. The flagpole – bent out of shape by the blast of the Eagle's engines when it had escaped back into space – had been straightened to preserve the image of the site as it had appeared on the old footage. But everything else was as it had been left: the descent stage of the lunar module, the instruments, even the astronauts' footprints. It was all surrounded by a towering steel wire fence topped with surveillance cameras: no one must get too near, trample on the sacred footprints of Armstrong and Aldrin, or carve their initials on the plaque attached to the leg of the descent stage.

A hushed silence now fell as the words on the plaque were quoted solemnly by the instructor: "Here men from the planet Earth first set foot up on the Moon. July 1969 A.D. We came in peace for all mankind."

First set foot on the Moon. Kate wondered how those two men must have felt when they first climbed out onto the lunar soil. Above them had been the same jet-black sky and sunlit Earth, about them the same barren, crater-strewn plain. But for those pioneering spacemen there had been no emergency response teams, no Luna Base with its decorative greenery and mall full of bright lit shops. No other living thing – not so much as a microbe – had shared the gray wasteland with them. The nearest human being had been the pilot in the orbiting command service module, high above. All the rest of humanity had been crowded into that cloud-swathed sphere nearly four hundred thousand kilometers away. Other explorers would follow over the years and feel that isolation in turn; but to be the *first* . . . Kate shivered. First to walk the gray solitudes, first to disturb the thick soft dust no wind had ever lifted . . . She realized suddenly that she had strayed somewhat and was now some distance away from the others. She turned hastily to rejoin them.

But there was a woman standing in the way.

Kate stared. It was not unusual for a stray tourist or maintenance worker to be out here on the lunar surface. But this woman was different.

She wasn't wearing a space suit.

She stood there as though the moon's airless surface were the most natural place for her to be: a slender woman, Asian-featured, wearing a kimono of some green silky material embroidered with flowers. There were real flowers in her hair – shell-pink blossoms nestling among ebony tresses piled neatly atop her head. About her neck there hung a string of lustrous, cream-colored pearls. The gaze of her large brown eyes was cool, solemn, and direct.

There were no footprints behind her, nor were there any shadows on the gray ground at her feet.

Kate's breath boomed like thunder inside her helmet. Her mouth was dry as a bone. The gravity that allowed the other students to leap and bound around the steel fence seemed to be binding her to the ground. As she stared helplessly, the woman in the green kimono approached. There was no smile of welcome on the delicate features; her expression was somber, her tread light but purposeful as she drew closer to Kate.

Kate longed desperately for something to break the spell. But fear and disbelief immobilized her. The pale woman was almost touching her; an arm in a long, flowing sleeve reached out towards Kate's faceplate. It stopped before actually making contact, the white hand raised in a gesture of . . . command? Entreaty? Kate could not take her eyes from the woman's; they were as deep as shadows, their gaze calm and compelling. She was willing Kate to do something. But what?

The hand gestured again. *Open your faceplate*, it said, as plain as speech.

Kate tried to swallow and couldn't.

Open it — let me touch you . . .

"No," Kate whispered. But it was only a croak.

The woman who was not — could not — really be there gazed at Kate steadily. The embroidered flowers upon her pale-green robe stood out in precise and minute detail, real as the harshly lit moon rocks, the granular patterns in the soil. Without speaking, the woman commanded her again. Her will reached out across the airless space like a lightning bolt arcing from cloud to cloud.

Raise your faceplate — now.

"Kate? KATE?"

At the sound of the voice, jarringly loud inside her helmet, Kate moved at last — straight upward, in a leap that would have cleared an Olympic high jump back on Earth. She spun, arms flailing, before falling slowly back to the lunar surface.

"Kate? Did I startle you? Sorry." It was the instructor; he was standing over her, peering out through his faceplate with a mixture of amusement and concern. Kate scrambled to her feet, grateful for his timely interruption – then she went rigid again, her heart hammering. The woman was still there, standing a few paces away.

The instructor couldn't see her.

Kate spoke with an effort. "I . . . I was just . . . daydreaming. And I . . ." Her voice faded away, for the woman was gliding silently toward her again, her eyes intent.

"We're heading back to the base now," the instructor told her.

She hastily joined him, springing along at his side. She wondered wildly for a moment if the ghostly woman would follow, join them in the shuttle's cramped interior, disembark with them, and wander about in the bright lit mall . . .

But a glance over her shoulder showed her only the flat and empty plain. The green-robed figure had vanished as though it had never been there at all.

"Want to come to the VR-cade with us, Kate?" one of the boys asked. "They've got some great new games."

Kate whirled, startled, to face the other students. "What? Oh . . . no, thanks. I think I'll just go to my quarters – I'm kind of tired."

"See you later then." The other kids moved away through the Lunar Mall in a noisy chattering group, gliding gracefully in the weak gravity. Kate was left alone.

She walked on through the mall in a daze. *It starts with hallucinations*, she thought. Matt had been right; she was going moon-mad. Only a crazy would come here to live, people on Earth said: social misfits, loners, eccentrics of all kinds – they ended up here, like a kind of flotsam cast up from Earth. Loony Lunies! But why should *she* suffer from moon-madness? She had only been here for three Earth months, and she'd been enjoying every minute of it. Now she recalled, with a pulse of horror, the woman in the strange robe with its intricate pattern of long-petaled flowers embroidered on the green material. They intruded on her vision, for a terrifying instant were clearer than the scene of shops and pedestrians around her.

No – go away!

She realized in alarm that she had almost said it out loud.

So much for sensible, scientific Kate Iwasaki! she thought bitterly. *I'll have to go to the counselor now, and he'll ship me home on the next shuttle.* She looked fearfully at the other shoppers. Surely they must see how tense and obviously agitated she was. She thought one or two of them looked at her oddly as they passed, and she hastily turned toward a storefront, pretending to admire the wares on display.

It was Ramachandra's gift shop. She'd often paused to gaze at the items in its display case, all beyond her own modest price range. Most souvenirs here were tacky and cheap: plastic models of shuttles or moon rocks with "A gift from Luna Base" emblazoned on them in gold letters. But Mr. Ramachandra sold quality goods. Loveliest of all were the little sculptures which he made himself: graceful figures and animal shapes that seemed to quiver with life. Kate pretended to examine one now, an elegant figure of a woman with a hunting bow in her hands. The string was of gold wire, the arrow poised and ready for flight. A hound stood at the woman's side, eager, ready to spring.

"Artemis, Goddess of the Moon," said a voice in her ear.

She looked up, and to her embarrassment found herself staring into the face of Mr. Ramachandra himself: an elderly Indian man, with white hair wisping around a bald, nut-brown scalp. He was attired, as always, in an outrageous many-colored robe adorned with bits of flashing mirror that glittered as he moved. His eyes were darkest brown, the color of black coffee.

She realized to her dismay that she was on the verge of tears, and that Mr. Ramachandra knew it.

"Something is wrong," he said in an undertone, making it a statement of fact rather than a question.

Kate gulped a lungful of air, furious with herself. "It's nothing," she managed to say, but the answer rang false even in her own ears.

"Oh, dear. *That* kind of nothing." He waved to a door at the back of his shop. "I was just going to have a cup of tea. Will you join me? Tea can be an excellent restorative."

She didn't really want to join him, but it was either that, or risk bawling in public like an idiot. *If I'm going to have to leave Luna Base, at least let me do it with some dignity*, she thought, and followed Mr. Ramachandra into the back room. It was small and cluttered, with half-finished figurines of stone, wood, or clay sitting on the shelves.

"I'll just put the kettle on," said Mr. Ramachandra. "There. Now perhaps you'd like to tell me what's wrong?"

"Oh, nothing really. I'm just going crazy, is all," she replied, smiling wanly.

"If so you're in the right place. Only a lunatic would go to the Moon. We are all a little bit odd, we Lunies, wouldn't you agree?"

"This is more than just being odd. I've got moon-madness." Tears welled in her eyes, and she blinked, hard. "Hallucinations and everything. They'll have to send me back home."

"What sort of hallucinations are you having?"

In a few short sentences she told him. It was easy to talk of it in here, with the kettle on the stove and the workroom all around her, small and cluttered and normal. Mr. Ramachandra raised his white eyebrows when she had finished.

"Curious," he said. He rose and went to the kettle, which was already shrieking for attention. He glanced at her thoughtfully over his shoulder. "You're Japanese, aren't you, Kate?" he added abruptly as he filled a teapot, waiting patiently as the water, slowed by the low gravity, slid down the kettle's spout like ketchup.

"Canadian, actually," she corrected.

"But you are Japanese by descent, am I right?"

"Yes," she admitted, wondering where this was leading.

"Curious," he said again. He settled in his chair as the tea steeped. "Are you familiar with Japanese folklore and legends?"

"Not really. I'm more into science."

"Then you'll not be familiar with the old tale of the maiden of the Moon?" She shook her head and he continued, a faraway look in his eyes, "There was once an old couple in long-ago Japan, who yearned for a child of their own. One day when the husband was cutting bamboo, he found a tiny human infant, a little girl, tucked away in one of the hollow stems. He and his wife raised this girl-child, and she grew into a beautiful maiden. But she would not marry any of the wealthy men who came to ask for her hand in marriage. She explained that she was a magical being, a child of the Moon, and one day she would have to return to her own people in the moon-world. And, indeed, there came a night when a company of glorious spirit people descended upon a moon-beam, and they bore the lovely moon-maiden away with them into the sky as her foster parents watched in sorrow." His coffee-colored eyes looked deep into hers. "You're quite sure you've never heard this story?"

Kate hesitated. "Pretty sure." She had, in fact, no recollection of it whatsoever.

"And yet your hallucination, as you call it, seems strongly reminiscent of it. Moon-people. Elegant spirit beings in a lunar realm. It almost makes one wonder if there might not be a kind of ancestral memory, or . . ."

"Or what?"

"Or perhaps what you saw was – real."

She stared. *He's the crazy one, not me*, she thought.

"The Moon," Ramachandra continued as he poured the tea into two large mugs, "the Moon is many things. It is a home for us, and a provider of useful resources. But it is also a place of myth and fable – a repository of dreams, if you will." His own face took on a dreamy look. "A land about which myths have been woven is a haunted place. How haunted must the Moon be, which hangs in the sky for all to see, which all cultures have held in common since the dawn of time!

"Among these empty wastes dwells the Chinese goddess Chang'o, in the form of an immortal toad; and the Man in the Moon wanders about with his bundle of sticks on his back and his faithful dog at his side; and the Maori woman Rona, exiled here after cursing the moon-god, gazes longingly at the Earth to which she can never return. For us Hindus, the Moon is associated with Soma, god of the sacred plant that brings ecstasy to mortals. I have felt positively blissful ever since I first arrived here.

"Now perhaps Mr. Ramachandra's mind is only making him believe that he feels the presence of the god. Perhaps that is the explanation. And then again," he added, with an impish smile, "perhaps it *isn't*."

She stared at him over her steaming mug. "What are you saying – that all those things are real?"

He answered with a question of his own. "Why did you come to Luna Base?"

She shrugged. "I guess I just wanted to see the Moon. It's always interested me."

"How so?"

"Oh, I don't know," she said irritably. "Is it important?"

"It might be." Mr Ramachandra sipped his tea and stared into space. "The original moon landings, now – why did those astronauts come here? It was quite pointless, from a sci-entific standpoint. It had already been demonstrated that automated machines could do the same thing more cheaply and with no risk to human life. But we are a romantic and impractical species, we humans."

Kate made a dismissive gesture. "My dad said it was all done for political reasons."

"The space race was, yes. But the desire to walk upon the Moon – that goes back further to the old myths and legends, to dreamers like Jules Verne. That is why the world watched and held its breath in 1969. And that is why some of us come here – not the tourists, who only want to do what the neigh-bors haven't done, to take pictures and jump higher than on Earth. No, it is the Moon of myth and magic that calls people like you and me."

"But if the woman I saw was . . . real, then everyone else should have seen her too," Kate argued.

"Maybe not, if it was a spirit you saw." He put down his mug and waved his arms about vaguely. "The spirit realm is everywhere, but it is not like our physical reality. It is differ-ent for each one of us, or so I believe."

Kate looked away. "I . . . would rather she wasn't real. You see, she wants me dead."

"Why do you say that?"

Kate rose and began to pace the little room. "She wanted me to open up my faceplate. To let all my air out, and die. She *wanted* that. I could see it, in her eyes."

"But you don't know why she would want such a thing?"

"No! That's just it. Why? What's it all about?" She was almost shouting now.

Mr. Ramachandra's voice and gaze remained calm. "Why don't you ask her?"

Kate stood tensely inside the main air lock, listening to her own short, sharp breaths. She'd have to be quick: students weren't allowed out on their own. The metal door slid open; there was a hiss of expelled air; and dust grains danced briefly before settling again. Before her lay smooth gray ground surrounded by barren hills: the desolate grandeur of the Taurus-Littrow Valley.

Kate drew a deep breath and leaped out of the air lock.

She bounded down the length of the valley, halting only when the safe comforting glow of the base was far behind her. A huge, gray-white boulder sprawled up ahead, casting a long shadow under the harsh sun. Kate paused next to it, and waited.

"Come on," she whispered. "Where are you?"

Nothing stirred. The valley was empty, as it had been for billions of years. Kate turned slowly, scanning the hills, the drab gray ground.

And then, quite suddenly, she noticed the tree.

It was no more than a few moon-strides away on the valley's flat floor, growing where nothing should be able to grow: a slender sapling covered in sharp-pointed leaves. As she stared at it, leaves and branches stirred, as though bending to the whim of a wind. The little tree bowed and swayed before her, offering no explanation for itself, a green intrusion on the moonscape.

Kate swallowed hard. *Hallucinations again.* She missed the Earth, with its green growing things, that was all. But the tree did not fade as she approached it. It looked so *real*. She must try to touch it, prove to herself that it wasn't actually there . . .

And then she halted in midstride, for the shapes of other trees were appearing all around her. Insubstantial at first, like smoke or shadow, their spindly forms solidified as she watched. The gray land around her bore a blush of green. Above her, blossoms hung amid the stars, clustering on the half-seen boughs of some flowering tree. She whirled. The great gray boulder was still there, but now its rugged sides were mottled with moss and lichen and surrounded by large-fronded ferns. The other rocks also remained where they had been, but they had changed. Random moon-rubble no longer, they formed part of a garden whose lush greenery they complemented, as if by design. A large, ornamental pond spread before her, a mirror for black sky and blue Earth; beside it stood a squat stone lantern, its peaked roof sheltering a flame that danced as it fed upon some other, alien air.

Then Kate saw the woman.

She was walking along the far side of the pool. Her jet-black hair now streamed loosely upon her shoulders, teased by the same wind that played in the little tree, and her robe was white. Where she walked, grass sprang from the regolith; it did not so much sprout as suddenly appear, as though her presence called it into being. And there was a path beneath her feet, a path lit by stone lanterns that ran winding into the hills beyond – hills that were rocky and barren no longer. On one jade-green summit there rose pagoda-roofed towers, their windows glowing warmly against the black sky.

The white-clad woman was now close enough to touch. Kate's blood turned to ice, but she held her ground. The woman raised one hand, gesturing gracefully.

Suddenly Kate understood.

She was being invited to join the woman: to go with her up the winding curves of that lamplit path, up into the hills that were empty no more. Up to the palace with its shining towers. There would be music and warmth within, and light and laughter; and something more, more than any of these things, something for which her heart hungered . . .

Kate set a booted foot upon the path, mesmerized. She would go. She would enter that palace, that place of light where a welcome awaited her. All that came between her and that realm was this heavy, cumbersome suit that she wore. It held her back, anchored her to the dead realm of the airless waste. She could cast it off, set it aside, be freed forever from the need for it.

Freed . . .

Understanding came to Kate in a blinding flash, and she halted in the middle of her second step. The woman in white turned to her, eyes inquiring. Kate made herself meet those deep tranquil eyes, boldly and directly.

"No," she said.

The sound of her voice could not reach the woman. Or could it? The dark eyes widened, the hovering hand fell. The woman faced her, eyes steady and intense, imposing her will.

"*No*," Kate said again, more forcefully. "I want to stay here. *Here*. Do you understand? I'm not going with you!"

The woman stared at her, first with gentle puzzlement, then with comprehension, which broke upon her face like a wave. For the first time her deep eyes smiled. She shook her head and laughed soundlessly. Then, in an instant, she was gone.

With her went all the life and color of that other world. Trees and shrubbery wisped away to nothingness; the Earth-reflecting pool rippled away like a heat mirage, and there in its place was the dry, gray ground. The far hills were bare and lifeless once more, the lofty towers bowed and faded. Of the garden only the boulders remained, forlorn as bare bones. Kate was alone once more. Her eyes misted, but only briefly.

She drew a sharp, shuddering breath. And headed back through the silent valley to Luna Base.

Mr. Ramachandra was modeling clay in his workshop. When he glanced up and saw Kate standing in the doorway, he smiled but said nothing, his fingers continuing to pinch and stroke the clay.

"I confronted her," she blurted.

He put the clay down. "Ah."

"You were right," said Kate. "Everything was all right. She didn't mean me any harm; she only wanted me to join her, in *her* world. I think she believed I wanted to. When I looked in her eyes, it was as though she understood. I don't think I'll ever see her again."

He tilted his head to one side, considering. "No, I don't suppose you will."

"So, what happened out there? Was she real? Or did it all just happen inside my head? Was I moon-mad, and did going out there cure me?"

He looked thoughtful. "If I were making up a story, I would say that your spirit came from the Moon; that you inhabited this sphere long before you were born in a human body. And that is why you longed for the Moon, like the maiden in the folktale, why you came here as soon as you had the chance. It was a homecoming, if you will. But you realized that to return to your spirit life, you would have to leave your human, physical life behind, together with your family and friends down on Earth. And you couldn't make yourself do that."

He rose and went to a shelf, taking from it a small figurine, which he held out to her. Kate stared at it: a woman in a flowing kimono, standing upon a base that curved like the crescent moon. "It's beautiful," she said shyly.

"It is the moon maiden from the story."

She reached out, ran a finger over the exquisite folds of the robe, the flying hair. "How . . . how much are you asking for it?"

He pressed the little figurine into her hands. "Consider it a gift," he said. "I do not charge my friends."

She thanked him, stammering a little, then met his dark brown eyes again. "You know, that was really dangerous, sending me out onto the surface all by myself. I might've cracked . . . flipped open my faceplate, or something. What made you so sure I'd be all right?"

He said nothing, but continued to gaze at her, calmly and confidently, a smile at the corners of his mouth.

"Thanks," she said awkwardly.

Then she turned and walked away, the moon maiden clutched in her hands.

What if ... you only got *one* wish?

A WISH NAMED ARNOLD
Charles de Lint

Marguerite kept a wish in a brass egg and its name was Arnold.

The egg screwed apart in the middle. Inside, wrapped in a small piece of faded velvet, was the wish. It was a small wish, about the length of a man's thumb, and was made of black clay in the rough shape of a bird. Marguerite decided straight away that it was a crow, even if it did have a splash of white on its head. That made it just more special for her, because she'd dyed a forelock of her own dark hair a peroxide white just before the summer started — much to her parents' dismay.

She'd found the egg under a pile of junk in Miller's while tagging along with her mother and aunt on their usual weekend tour of the local antique shops. Miller's was near their cottage on Otty Lake, just down the road from Rideau Ferry, and considered to be the best antique shop in the area.

The egg and its dubious contents were only two dollars, and maybe the egg was dinged-up a little and didn't screw together quite right, and maybe the carving didn't look so much like a crow as it did a lump of black clay with what could be a beak on it, but she'd bought it all the same.

It wasn't until Arnold talked to her that she found out he was a wish.

"What do you mean you're a wish?" she'd asked, keeping her voice low so that her parents wouldn't think she'd taken to talking in her sleep. "Like a genie in a lamp?"

Something like that.

It was all quite confusing. Arnold lay in her hand, an unmoving lump that was definitely not alive even if he did look like a bird, sort of. That was a plain fact, as her father liked to say. On the other hand, someone was definitely speaking to her in a low buzzing voice that tickled pleasantly inside her head.

I wonder if I'm dreaming, she thought.

She gave her white forelock a tug, then brushed it away from her brow and bent down to give the clay bird a closer look.

"What sort of a wish can you give me?" she asked finally.

Think of something — any one thing that you want — and I'll give it to you.

"Anything?"

Within reasonable limits.

Marguerite nodded sagely. She was all too familiar with *that* expression. "Reasonable limits" was why she only had one forelock dyed instead of a whole swath of rainbow colors like her friend Tina, or a Mohawk like Sheila. If she just washed her hair and let it dry, *and* you ignored the dyed forelock, she had a most reasonable short haircut. But all it took was a little gel that she kept hidden in her purse and by the time she joined her friends at the mall, her hair was sticking out around her head in a bristle of spikes. It was just such a pain wearing a hat when she came home and having to wash out the gel right away.

Maybe that should be her wish. That she could go around looking just however she pleased and nobody could tell her any different. Except that seemed like a waste of a wish. She should probably ask for great heaps of money and jewels. Or maybe for a hundred more wishes.

"How come I only get one wish?" she asked.

Because that's all I am, Arnold replied. *One small wish.*

"Genies and magic fish give three. In fact *everybody* in *all* the stories usually gets three. Isn't it a tradition or something?"

Not where I come from.

"Where do you come from?"

There was a moment's pause, then Arnold said softly, *I'm not really sure.*

Marguerite felt a little uncomfortable at that. The voice tickling her mind sounded too sad and she started to feel ashamed of being so greedy.

"Listen," she said. "I didn't really mean to . . . you know . . ."

That's all right, Arnold replied. *Just let me know when you've decided what your wish is.*

Marguerite got a feeling in her head then, as though something had just slipped away, like a lost memory or a half-remembered thought, then she realized that Arnold had just gone back to wherever it was that he'd been before she'd opened the egg. Thoughtfully, she wrapped him up in the faded velvet, then shut him away in the egg. She put the egg under her pillow and went to sleep.

All the next day she kept thinking about the brass egg and the clay crow inside it, about her one wish and all the wonderful things that there were to wish for. She meant to take out the egg right away, first thing in the morning, but she never quite found the time. She went fishing with her father after breakfast, and then she went into Perth to shop with her mother, and then she went swimming with Steve who lived two cottages down and liked punk music as much as she did, though maybe for different reasons. She didn't get back to her egg until bedtime that night.

"What happens to you after I've made my wish?" she asked after she'd taken Arnold out of the egg.

I go away.

Marguerite asked, "Where to?" before she really thought about what she was saying, but this time Arnold didn't get upset.

To be someone else's wish, he said.

"And after that?"

Well, after they've made their wish, I'll go on to the next and the next . . .

"It sounds kind of boring."

Oh, no. I get to meet all sorts of interesting people.

Marguerite scratched her nose. She'd gotten a mosquito bite right on the end of it and felt very much like Pinocchio though she hadn't been telling any lies.

"Have you always been a wish?" she asked, not thinking again.

Arnold's voice grew so quiet that it was just a feathery touch in her mind. *I remember being something else . . . a long time ago . . .*

Marguerite leaned closer, as though that would help her hear him better. But there was a sudden feeling in her, as though Arnold had shaken himself out of his reverie.

Do you know what you're going to wish for yet? he asked briskly.

"Not exactly."

Well, just let me know when you're ready, he said and then he was gone again.

Marguerite sighed and put him away. This didn't seem to be at all the way this whole wishing business should go. Instead of feeling all excited about being able to ask for any one thing – *anything!* – she felt guilty because she kept making Arnold feel bad. Mind you, she thought, he did seem to be a gloomy sort of a genie when you came right down to it.

She fell asleep wondering if he looked the same wherever he went to when he left her as he did when she held him in her hand. Somehow his ticklish raspy voice didn't quite go with the lumpy clay figure that lay inside the brass egg. She supposed she'd never know.

As the summer progressed they became quite good friends, in an odd sort of way. Marguerite took to carrying the egg around with her in a small quilted bag that she slung over her shoulder. At opportune moments, she'd take Arnold out and they'd talk about all sorts of things.

Arnold, Marguerite discovered, knew a lot that she hadn't supposed a genie would know. He was current with all the latest bands, seemed to have seen all the best movies, knew stories that could make her giggle uncontrollably or shiver with chills under her blankets late at night. If she didn't press him for information about his past, he proved to be the best friend a person could want and she found herself telling him things she'd never think of telling anyone else.

It got to the point where Marguerite forgot he was a wish. Which was fine until the day that she left her quilted cotton bag behind in a restaurant in Smiths Falls on a day's outing with her mother. She became totally panic-stricken until her mother took her back to the restaurant, but by then her bag was gone, and so was the egg, and with it Arnold.

Marguerite was inconsolable. She moped around for days and nothing that anyone could do could cheer her up. She missed Arnold passionately. Missed their long talks when she was supposed to be sleeping. Missed the weight of his egg in her shoulder bag and the companionable presence of just knowing he was there. And also, she realized, she'd missed her chance of using her wish.

She could have had anything she wanted. She could have asked for piles of money. For fame and fortune. To be a lead singer in a rock band. To be a famous actor and star in all kinds of movies. She could have wished that Arnold would stay with her forever. Instead, jerk that she was, she'd never used the wish and now she had nothing. How could she be so stupid?

"Oh," she muttered one night in her bed. "I wish . . . I wish . . ."

She paused then, feeling a familiar tickle in her head.

Did you finally decide on your wish? Arnold asked.

Marguerite sat up so suddenly that she knocked over her water glass on the night table. Luckily it was empty.

"Arnold?" she asked, looking around. "Are you here?"

Well, not exactly here, *as it were, but I can hear you.*

"Where have you been?"

Waiting for you to make your wish.

"I've really missed you," Marguerite said. She patted her comforter with eager hands, trying to find Arnold's egg. "How did you get back here?"

I'm not exactly here, Arnold said.

"How come you never talked to me when I've been missing you all this time?"

I really can't initiate these things, Arnold explained. *It gets rather complicated, but even though my egg's with someone else, I can't really be their wish until I've finished being yours.*

"So we can still talk and be friends even though I've lost the egg?"

Not exactly. I can fulfill your wish, but since I'm not with you, as it were, I can't really stay unless you're ready to make your wish.

"You can't?" Marguerite wailed.

Afraid not. I don't make the rules, you know.

"I've got it," Marguerite said. And she did have it too. If she wanted to keep Arnold with her, all she had to do was wish for him to always be her friend. Then no one could take him away from her. They'd always be together.

"I wish . . ." she began.

But that didn't seem quite right, she realized. She gave her bleached forelock a nervous tug. It wasn't right to *make* someone be your friend. But if she didn't do that, if she wished something else, then Arnold would just go off and be somebody else's wish. Oh, if only things didn't have to be so complicated. Maybe she should just wish herself to the moon and be done with all her problems. She could lie there and stare at the world from a nice long distance away while she slowly asphyxiated. That would solve everything.

She felt that telltale feeling in her mind that let her know that Arnold was leaving again.

"Wait," she said. "I haven't made my wish yet."

The feeling stopped. *Then you've decided?* Arnold asked.

She hadn't, but as soon as he asked, she realized that there was only one fair wish she could make.

"I wish you were free," she said.

The feeling that was Arnold moved blurrily inside her.

You what? he asked.

"I wish you were free. I *can* wish that, can't I?"

Yes, but . . . Wouldn't you rather have something . . . well, something for yourself?

"This *is* for myself," Marguerite said. "Your being free would be the best thing I could wish for because you're my friend and I don't want you to be trapped anymore." She paused for a moment, brow wrinkling. "Or is there a rule against that?"

No rule, Arnold said softly. His ticklish voice bubbled with excitement. *No rule at all against it.*

"Then that's my wish," Marguerite said.

Inside her mind, she felt a sensation like a tiny whirlwind spinning around and around. It was like Arnold's voice and an autumn leaves smell and a kaleidoscope of dervishing lights, all wrapped up in one whirling sensation.

Free! Arnold called from the center of that whirligig. *Free free free!*

A sudden weight was in Marguerite's hand and she saw that the brass egg had appeared there. It lay open in her palm, the faded velvet spilled out of it. It seemed so very small to hold so much happiness, but fluttering on tiny wings was the clay crow, rising up in a spin that twinned Arnold's presence in Marguerite's mind.

Her fingers closed around the brass egg as Arnold doubled, then tripled his size in an explosion of black feathers. His voice was like a chorus of bells, ringing and ringing between Marguerite's ears. Then with an exuberant caw, he stroked the air with his wings, flew out the cottage window, and was gone.

Marguerite sat quietly, staring out the window and holding the brass egg. A big grin stretched her lips. There was something so *right* about what she'd just done that she felt an overwhelming sense of happiness herself, as though she'd been the one trapped in a treadmill of wishes in a brass egg, and Arnold had been the one to free *her*.

At last she reached out and picked up from the comforter a small glossy black feather that Arnold had left behind. Wrapping it in the old velvet, she put it into the brass egg and screwed the egg shut once more.

That September a new family moved in next door with a boy her age named Arnold. Marguerite was delighted and, though her parents were surprised, she and the new boy became best friends almost immediately. She showed him the egg one day that winter and wasn't at all surprised that the feather she still kept in it was the exact same shade of black as her new friend's hair.

Arnold stroked the feather with one finger when she let him see it. He smiled at her and said, "I had a wish once . . ."

MUFFIN EXPLAINS TELEOLOGY
TO THE WORLD AT LARGE

James Alan Gardner

I told my kid sister Muffin this joke.

There was this orchestra, and they were playing music, and all the violins were bowing and moving their fingers, except for this one guy who just played the same note over and over again. Someone asked the guy why he wasn't playing like the others and he said, "They're all looking for the note. I've found it."

Muffin, who's only six, told me the joke wasn't funny if you understood teleology.

I never know where she gets words like that. I had to go and look it up.

teleology [teli-oloji] *n*. doctrine or theory that all things or processes were designed to fill a purpose.

"Okay," I said when I found her again, "now I understand teleology. Why isn't the joke funny?"

"You'll find out next week," she said.

I talked to Uncle Dave that night. He's in university and real smart, even though he's going to be a minister instead of something interesting. "What's so great about teleology?" I said. He looked at me kind of weird so I explained, "Muffin's been talking about it."

"So have my professors," he said. "It's, uhh, you know, God has a purpose for everything, even if we can't understand it. We're all heading towards some goal."

"We took that in Sunday School," I said.

"Well, Jamie, we go into it in a bit more detail."

"Yeah, I guess."

He was quiet for a bit, then asked, "What's Muffin say about it?"

"Something big is happening next week."

"Teleologically speaking?"

"That's what she says."

Muffin was in the next room with her crayons. Uncle Dave called her in to talk and she showed him what she was working on. She'd colored Big Bird black. She has all these crayons and the only ones she ever uses are black and gray.

"What's happening next week?" Uncle Dave asked.

"It's a secret," she said.

"Not even a hint?"

"No."

"Little tiny hint? Please?"

She thought about it a minute, then whispered in his ear. Then she giggled and ran upstairs.

"What did she say?" I asked.

"She said that we'd get where we were going." He shrugged and made a face. We were both pretty used to Muffin saying things we didn't understand.

The next day, I answered the front doorbell and found three guys wearing gray robes. They'd shaved their heads too.

"We are looking for her gloriousness," one of them said with a little bow. He had an accent.

"Uh, Mom's gone down the block to get some bread," I answered.

"It's okay," Muffin said, coming from the TV room. "They're here for me."

All three of the men fell face down on the porch making a kind of high whining sound in their throats. "You know these guys?" I asked.

"They're here to talk about teleology."

"Oh. Well, take them around to the backyard. Mom doesn't like people in the house when she's not here."

"Okay." She told the guys to get up and they followed her around the side of the house, talking in some foreign language.

When Mom got home, I told her what happened and she half-ran to the kitchen window to see what was going on. Muffin was sitting on the swing set and the guys were cross-legged on the ground in front of her, nodding their heads at every word she spoke. Mom took a deep breath, the way she does just before she's going to yell at one of us, then stomped out the back door. I was sure she was going to shout at Muffin, but she bent over and talked quiet enough that I couldn't hear from inside the house. Muffin talked and Mom talked and one of the bald guys said something, and finally Mom came in all pale-looking.

"They want lemonade," she said. "Take them out some lemonade. And plastic glasses. I'm going to lie down." And she went upstairs.

I took them out a pitcher of lemonade. When I got there, one of the bald guys got up to meet me and asked Muffin, "Is this the boy?"

She said yes.

"Most wondrous, most wondrous!"

He put both hands on my shoulders as if he was going to hug me, but Muffin said, "You'll spill the lemonade." He let me go, but kept staring at me with his big, weepy, white eyes.

"What's going on?" I asked.

"The culmination of a thousand thousand years of aimless wandering," the guy said.

"Not aimless," Muffin cut in.

"Your pardon," he answered, quickly lowering his head. "But at times it seemed so."

"You'll be in the temple when it happens," Muffin said to him.

"A million praises!" he shouted, throwing himself flat-faced on the ground. "A billion trillion praises!" And he started to cry into our lawn. The other two bowed in the direction of our garage, over and over again.

"You want to pour me a glass of that?" Muffin said to me.

The next day, Muffin told me I had to take her down to the boatyards. I said, "I don't have to do anything."

"Shows how much you know," she answered. "You don't know anything about teleology or fate or anything."

"I know how to cross streets and take buses and all, which is more than I can say for some people."

"I have ten dollars," she said, pulling a bill out of the pocket of her jeans.

That surprised me. I mean, I maybe have ten dollars in my pocket twice a year, just after Christmas and just after my birthday. "Where'd you get the money?" I asked.

"The monks gave it to me."

"Those bald guys?"

"They like me."

"Geez, Muffin, don't let Mom know you took money from strangers. She'd have a fit."

"They aren't strangers. They're the Holy Order of the Imminent Eschaton — the Muffin Chapter."

"Oh, go ahead, lie to me."

"You want the ten dollars or not?"

Which wasn't what I ended up with, because she expected me to pay the bus fare out of it.

When we got to the boatyards, I thought we'd head right down to the water, but Muffin just took out a piece of paper and stood there frowning at it. I looked over her shoulder and saw it was torn from a map of the city. There was a small red X drawn in at a place about a block from where we were. "Where'd you get that? The monks?"

"Mm-hm. Is this where we are?" She pointed at a corner. I looked and moved her finger till it pointed to the right place. "You should learn to read some time, Muffin."

She shook her head. "Might wreck my insight. Maybe after."

I pointed down the street. "If you want to go where X marks the spot, it's that way."

We walked along with sailboats and yachts and things on one side, and warehouses on the other. The buildings looked pretty run down, with brown smears of rust dripping down from their metal roofs, and lots of broken windows covered with plywood or cardboard. It was a pretty narrow street and there was no sidewalk, but the only traffic we saw was a Shell oil truck coming out of the Marina a ways ahead and it turned off before it got to us.

When we reached the X spot, the only thing there was another warehouse. Muffin closed her eyes for a second, then said, "Around the back and up the stairs."

"I bet there are rats around the back," I said.

"I bet there aren't."

"You go first."

"Okay." She started off down an alley between the one warehouse and the next. There was a lot of broken glass lying around and grass growing up through the pavement.

"I bet there are snakes," I said, following her.

"Shut up, Jamie," she said.

The back was only a strip of weeds about two yards wide, stuck between the warehouse and a chain-link fence. Halfway along, there was a flight of metal steps like a fire escape leading up to the roof. They creaked a bit when you walked on them, but didn't wobble too badly.

On the roof we found a really weird looking airplane. Or boat. Or train. Or wagon. Anyway, it had wings and tail like an airplane, but its body was built like a boat, a bit like the motorboat up at the cottage, but bigger and with those super-fat padded chairs like maybe astronauts sit in. The whole thing sat on a cart, but the cart's wheels were on the near end of a train track that ran the length of the roof and off the front into the street.

"What is this thing?" I asked.

"The monks made it for me," Muffin said, which didn't answer my question. She climbed up a short metal ladder into the plane and rummaged about in a cupboard in the rear wall. I followed her and watched her going through stuff inside. "Peanut butter. Bread. Kool-Aid. Water. Cheese. Diet Coke. What's this?" she said, handing me back a roll of something in gold plastic wrapping.

I opened one end and sniffed. "Liverwurst," I said.

"Is that like liver?" She made a face.

"No, it's sort of like peanut butter, but made from bologna."

"Weird. Do you see any hot dogs?"

I looked in the cupboard. "Nope."

"I should phone the monks. We need hot dogs."

"What for?"

She ignored me. "Is there anything else you'd want if you knew you were going to be away from home for a few days?"

"Cheerios and bacon."

She thought about that. "Yeah, you're right."

"And Big Macs."

She gave me a look like I was a moron. "Of course, dummy, but the monks will bring them just before we leave."

"We're going on a trip?"

"We're on a trip now. We're going to *arrive*."

Early the next morning, Dr. Hariki showed up on our doorstep all excited. He works with my dad at the university. My dad teaches physics; he works with lasers and everything. Dr. Hariki is in charge of the big telescope on the top of the Physics building, and he takes pictures of stars.

"What's up?" Dad asked.

"You tell me," Dr. Hariki said, spreading out a bunch of photographs on the coffee table.

Dad picked up a picture and looked at it. Turned it over to check out the date and time written on the back. Sorted through the stack of photos till he found whatever he was looking for and compared the two. Held the two together side by side. Held one above the other. Put them side by side again. Closed his right eye, then quick closed his left and opened his right. Did that a couple of times. Picked up another pair of photos and did the same.

Muffin came into the room with a glass of orange juice in her hand. "Looks more like a dipper now, doesn't it?" she said without looking at the pictures.

Dad and Dr. Hariki stared at her. "Well, it was a bit too spread out before, wasn't it?" she asked. "Don't you think it looks better now?"

"Muffin," Dad said, "we're talking about stars . . . suns. They don't just move about to make a nicer pattern."

"No, but if they're going to stop moving, you might as well make sure they look like a dipper in the end. Anything else is just sloppy. I mean, really."

She walked off into the TV room and a moment later we heard the *Sesame Street* theme song.

After a long silence, Dr. Hariki picked up one of the photographs and asked, all quiet, "Something to do with entropy?"

"I think it's teleology," I said.

That night Uncle Dave was over for Sunday supper. Mom figures that Uncle Dave doesn't eat so good in residence, so she feeds him a roast of something every Sunday. I think this is a great idea, except that every so often she serves squash because she thinks it's a delicacy. Lucky for us, it was corn season so we had corn on the cob instead.

After supper we all played Monopoly and I won. Uncle Dave said it made a nice family picture, us all sitting around the table playing a game. "Some day, kids," he said, "you're going to like having times like this to remember. A perfect frozen moment."

"There are all kinds of perfect frozen moments," Muffin said, and she had that tone in her voice like she was eleventy-seven years old instead of six. "Right now, people all over the world are doing all kinds of things. Like in China, it's day now, right Dad?"

"Right, Muffin."

"So there are kids playing tag and stuff, and that's a perfect moment. And maybe there's some bully beating up a little kid, and punching him out right now." She banged her Monopoly piece (the little metal hat) when she said 'now.' "And that's a perfect moment because that's what really happens. And bus drivers are driving their buses, and farmers are milking their cows, and mommies are kissing daddies, and maybe a ship is sinking some place. If you could take pictures of everyone right now, you'd see millions of perfect little frozen moments, wouldn't you?"

Uncle Dave patted Muffin's hand. "Out of the mouths of babes . . . I'm the one who's studying to appreciate the great wonders of Life, and you're the one who reminds me. Everything is perfect all the time, isn't it, Muffin?"

"Of course not, dummy," she answered, looking at Uncle Dave the way she did when he tried to persuade her he'd pulled a dime out of her ear. She turned around in her chair and reached over to the buffet to get the photograph they'd taken of her kindergarten class just before the summer holidays started. "See?" she said, pointing. "This is Bobby and he picks his nose all the time, and he's picking his nose here, so that's good. But this is Wendy, with her eyes closed cuz she was blinking. That's not perfect. Wendy cries every time she doesn't get a gold star in spelling, and she knows three dirty words, and she always gives Matthew the celery from her lunch, but you can't tell that from the picture, can you? She's just someone who blinked at the wrong time. If you want someone who should be blinking, it should be dozy old Peter Morgan who's fat and sweats and laughs funny."

Uncle Dave scratched his head and looked awkward for a bit, then said, "Well, Muffin, when you put it like that . . . yes, I suppose there are always some things that aren't aesthetically pleasing . . . I mean, there are always some things that don't fit properly, as you say."

"Not always," she said.

"Not always? Some day things are just suddenly going to be right?" Uncle Dave asked.

Muffin handed me the dice and said, "Your turn, Jamie. Bet you're going to land in jail."

Next morning, Muffin joggled my arm to wake me up. It was so early that the sun was just starting to rise over the lake. "Time to go down to the boatyards."

"Again?"

"Yep. This time for real." So I got up and dressed as quietly as I could. By the time I got down to the kitchen, Muffin had made some peanut butter and jam sandwiches, and was messing about with the waxed paper, trying to wrap them. She had twice as much paper as she needed and was making a botch of things.

"You're really clueless sometimes," I said, whispering so Mom and Dad wouldn't hear. I shoved her out of the way and started wrapping the sandwiches myself.

"When I rule the world, there won't be any waxed paper," she sulked.

We were halfway down to the bus stop when Uncle Dave came running up behind us. He had been staying the night in the guest room and I suppose he heard us moving around.

"Where do you think you're going?" he asked, and he was a bit mad at us.

"Down to the boatyards," Muffin said.

"No, you aren't. Get back to the house."

"Uncle Dave," Muffin said, "it's time."

"Time for what?"

"The Eschaton."

"Where do you pick up these words, Muffin? You're talking about the end of the world."

"I know." The first bus of the day was just turning onto our street two corners down. "Come to the boatyards with us, Uncle Dave. It'll be okay."

Uncle Dave thought about it. I guess he decided it was easier to give in than fight with her. That's what I always think too. You can't win an argument with her, and if you try anything else, she bites and scratches and uses her knees. "All right," Uncle Dave said, "but we're going to phone your parents and tell them where you are, the first chance we get."

"So talk to me about the Eschaton," Uncle Dave said on the bus. We were the only ones on it except for a red-haired lady wearing a Donut Queen uniform.

"Well," Muffin said, thinking things over, "you know how Daddy talks about everything moving in astronomy? Like the moon goes around the sun and the sun moves with the stars in the galaxy and the galaxy is moving too?"

"Yes . . ."

"Well, where is everything going?"

Uncle Dave shrugged. "The way your father tells it, everything just moves, that's all. It's not going anywhere in particular."

"That's stupid. Daddy doesn't understand teleology. Everything's heading for where it's supposed to end up."

"And what happens when things reach the place where they're supposed to end up?"

Muffin made an exasperated face. "They *end up* there."

"They stop?"

"What else would they do?"

"All the planets and the stars and all?"

"Mm-hm."

"People too?"

"Sure."

He thought for a second. "In perfect frozen moments, right?"

"Right."

Uncle Dave leaned his head against the window like he was tired and sad. Maybe he was. The sun was coming up over the housetops now. "Bus drivers driving their buses," he said softly, "and farmers milking their cows . . . the whole world like a coffee table book."

"I think you'd like to be in a church, Uncle Dave," Muffin said. "Or maybe walking alone along the lakeshore."

"Maybe," he smiled, all sad. Then he looked my sister right in the eye and asked, "Who are you, Muffin?"

"I'm me, dummy," she answered, throwing her arms around his neck and giving him a kiss.

He left us in front of the warehouse by the lake. "I'm going to walk down to the Rowing Club and back." He laughed a little. "If I get back, Muffin, you are going to get such a spanking . . ."

"Bye, Uncle Dave," she said, hugging him.

I hugged him too. "Bye, Uncle Dave."

"Don't let her do anything stupid," he said to me before heading down the street. We watched for a while, but he didn't turn back.

Up on the warehouse roof, there was a monk waiting with a McDonald's bag under his arm. He handed it to Muffin, then kneeled. "Bless me, Holy One."

"You're blessed," she said after looking in the bag. "Now get going to the temple or the airport or something. There's only about ten minutes left."

The monk hurried off, singing what I think was a hymn. We got into the plane-boat and I helped Muffin strap herself into one of the big padded seats. "The thing is," she said, "when the earth stops turning, we're going to keep on going."

"Hey, I know about momentum," I answered. I mean, Dad *is* a physicist.

"And it's going to be real fast, so we have to be sure we don't run into any buildings."

"We're going to shoot out over the lake?"

"We're high enough to clear the tops of the sailboats, then we just fly over the lake until we're slow enough to splash down. The monks got scientists to figure everything out."

I strapped myself in and thought about things for a while. "If we go shooting off real fast, isn't it going to hurt? I mean, the astronauts get all pressed down when they lift off . . ."

"Geez!" Muffin groaned. "Don't you know the difference between momentum and acceleration? Nothing's happening to us, it's everything else that's doing weird stuff. We don't feel a thing."

"Not even the wind?"

"The air has the same momentum we do, dummy."

I thought about it some more. "Aren't the buildings going to get wrecked when the earth stops?"

"They're going to stop too. Everything's just going to freeze except us."

"The air and the water are going to freeze too?"

"In spots. But not where we're going."

"We're special?"

"We're special."

Suddenly there was a roar like roller coaster wheels underneath us and for a moment I was pressed up against the straps holding me down on the seat. Then the pressure stopped and there was nothing but the sound of the wind a long way off. Over the side of the boat I could see water rushing by beneath us. We were climbing.

"Muffin," I asked. "Should one of us maybe be piloting this thing?"

"It's got a gyroscope or something. The monks worked absolutely everything out, okay?"

"Okay."

A long way off to the right, I could see a lake freighter with a curl of smoke coming out of its stack. The smoke didn't move. It looked neat. "Nice warm day," I said.

After a while, we started playing car games to pass the time.

The sun shone but didn't move. "If the sun stays there forever," I asked, "Won't it get really hot after a while?"

"Nah," Muffin answered. "It's some kind of special deal. I mean, it's not the same if you set up a nice picture of a park full of kids and then it gets hot as Mercury."

"Who's going to know?"

"It's not the same," she insisted.

"How can we see?"

"What do you mean?"

"Well, is the light moving or what?"

"It's another special deal."

That made sense. From the way Dad talked about physics, light was always getting special deals.

The water below us gradually stopped racing away so fast and we could sometimes see frozen whitecaps on the peaks of frozen waves. "Suppose we land on frozen water," I said.

"We won't."

"Oh. Your turn."

"I spy with my little eye something that begins with B." Right away I knew she meant the Big Macs, but I had to pretend it was a toughie. You have to humor little kids.

We splashed down within sight of a city on the far side of the lake. It was a really good splash, like the one on the Zoomba Flume ride when you get to the bottom of the big, long, water chute. Both of us got drenched. I was kind of sad there was no way to do it again.

Then I thought to myself, maybe if we were getting a special deal on air and water and heat and all, maybe we'd get a special deal on the Zoomba Flume too.

We unstrapped ourselves and searched around a bit. Finally, we found a lid that slid back to open up a control panel with a little steering wheel and all. We pushed buttons until an inboard motor started in the water behind us, then took turns driving towards shore. Every now and then we'd see a gull frozen in the sky, wings spread out and looking great.

We put in at a public beach just outside the city. It had been early in the day and the only people in sight were a pair of joggers on a grassy ridge that ran along the edge of the sand. The man wore only track shorts and sunglasses; the woman wore red stretch pants, a T-shirt, and a headband. Both had Walkmans and were stopped in midstride. Both had deep dark tans and, as Muffin pointed out, a thin covering of sweat.

I wanted to touch one to see what they felt like, but when my finger got close, it bumped up against an invisible layer of frozen air. The air didn't feel like anything, it was just solid stuff.

Down at one end of the beach, a teenage girl was frozen in the act of unlocking the door to a snack stand. We squeezed past her and found out that we could open the freezer inside. Muffin had a couple of Popsicles, I had an ice-cream sandwich, and then we went swimming.

Lying out in the sun afterwards, I asked Muffin what was going to happen next.

"You want to go swimming again?" she asked.

"No, I mean after."

"Let's eat," she said, dragging me back towards the boat.

"You can't wiggle out of it that easy," I told her. "Are we the only ones left?"

"I think so."

"Then are we going to freeze too?"

"Nope. We got a special deal."

"But it seems pretty stupid if you ask me. Everything's kind of finished, you know? Show's over. Why are we still hanging around?"

"For a new show, dummy."

"Oh," that made sense. "Same sort of thing?"

"We'll see."

"Oh. Where do *we* fit in?"

Muffin smiled at me. "You're here to keep me company."

"And what are you here for?"

"Everything else. Get me a sandwich."

So I reached down into the basket we'd brought and pulled one out. It was inside a plastic sandwich bag. "Didn't we put these in wax paper?" I asked.

Muffin smiled.

What if . . . the last snow leopard
on Earth were threatened?

THE ROAD TO SHAMBHALA

Eileen Kernaghan

Jang looked up, startled, as the woman's shadow fell across the light. Practicing his magic, he had been making a handful of walnut shells dance in midair. Now they dropped with a clatter to the floor.

"A good trick," said the woman. She unbuckled her pack and sat down on the teahouse bench, folding her long legs under her. "Food?" she inquired.

Jang brought her a plate of rice and lentils. Then he sat quietly on his heels and watched her eat. Dark-haired and deeply tanned, she was dressed like any villager, in loose shirt and trousers and wide palm-leaf hat. But she was too tall, too heavy-boned to be Nepalese, and her eyes were a vivid turquoise blue.

When she had finished eating she beckoned to Jang. "Is there anyone here who will sell me a packhorse?" she asked.

Immediately he thought of the brown pony belonging to his sister's husband Malla. "Oh, yes, Lady," he said. "A most excellent horse. I will arrange it."

Outside, the autumn morning was hot and clear. To the north the great white snow peaks, the wall at the world's end, marched against the sky.

Jang ran to his sister's hut to fetch his brother-in-law and the little shaggy hill pony. The stranger drove a shrewd bargain, and her hands, as she examined the pony, were sure and clever.

"Wait," said Jang, when the deal was struck. "Are you leaving now?"

"As soon as I've bought supplies."

"I will help you," Jang declared. "What is your name, please"

"Vale," said the woman, looking amused.

"So, Lady . . . Vale. Come with me. I will show you the best places in the bazaar."

She bought saddle bags, kettles and pans, lentils, rice, tea, stove oil. When the pony was loaded she dug into a pocket and handed Jang a coin. He sucked in his breath. It was the most money he had ever held in his hand at one time.

Clearly, this woman was rich. And she was traveling alone, into the hills.

"I will come with you," Jang said. "You will need a guide."

"I'm used to finding my own way," the woman said. "And don't you already have a job?"

"I work for my cousin, Lady. He will not mind."

It was a lie . . . his cousin would beat him soundly for running off. But it was no matter. If things went as he hoped, he would never see this village, or the teahouse, or his cousin again.

"I am strong," Jang insisted. "I can walk all day without stopping to rest, and I eat very little. It is not safe for you to go into the mountains alone. There are wolves. There are bandits."

"And will you protect me, Jang? Well, your offer is generous. But as you see, there is scarcely room in this small tent for myself."

"I can sleep on the bare ground," he said. "I have done it before."

"When was that?"

"Only last week. I was following a hunting party. They hired some men of our village as porters, but they said I was too young." He did not mention the tall man with the cold pale eyes and the sun-colored beard who had shouted at him and threatened him with a rifle; who had fired over his head as he fled down the steep mountain trail.

Turning away towards the river road, the woman said, "But they sent you back . . . and if you follow me, I'll do the same."

Jang returned to the teahouse. Creeping into the storeroom, he snatched up some dried figs and hid them in his blanket coat. Then, unnoticed by anyone, he slipped out the back door. By midday he was on the gray road leading north.

Soon the valley narrowed, terraced rice paddies giving way to bleak eroded hills. Jang's hill-born grandmother remembered a time when mossy oakwoods covered these wind-scoured slopes. "Where are the forests?" she would ask. "Where are the birds, the animals? Why has everything changed?" To which Jang's aunt Subha, who had been to school in the city, would reply, "You cannot stop things changing, Ama. Remember it is the twenty-first century, now. It is not only Nepal, but the whole world, that has changed."

And Jang's other grandmother, who came from the southern plains, would shake her head, and wring her hands, lamenting, "Truly, children, we are living in the Kali Yuga, the Last Age of the World."

Jang overtook the woman in a high meadow just as she was preparing to move off. "Lady," he gasped, as he slithered headlong down the steep hill track. "Wait for me, Lady."

She turned and stared at him. Jang took a deep breath, gathered his wits and his dignity about him. "You see," he said, "how fast I travel. I will be no hindrance to you."

The woman said, "I can see you are foolish, and a bad listener to boot."

"I will work hard for you, Lady. I will feed the pony, and make your tea, and cook your rice. And I can do many kinds of magic. For example, the spell for conjuring fire . . ."

But she was only half-listening. In desperation, he declared, "I would work twice as hard for you, Lady, as for the yellow-bearded one."

He heard the sudden sharp intake of her breath.

"What did you say? What yellow-bearded one?"

Puzzled, he said, "Why, the man I followed before, who drove me away with his gun."

"Describe this man."

Jang said, "I think he was very rich – a prince maybe. He had fine clothes, and gold threads plaited into his beard. And I remember thinking, for all his handsome looks, this is a very bad man, a wicked man. His eyes were cruel."

"Yes," said the woman. "You've described him well. He calls himself Goldbeard. He's very rich. And very wicked. And he's come to Nepal to kill the last snow leopard."

"But they are all dead," said Jang. Surely the last of the great white cats – like the blue sheep, the moon-bear and the red panda – had vanished in his grandmother's time.

"All but one," Vale replied. "Somewhere in these hills, one survives – the most solitary and the most elusive of beasts. And because it *is* the last, Goldbeard is determined to kill it."

"Why?" None of this made the slightest sense to Jang.

"Because," said Vale, "it's Goldbeard's obsession to track down and kill the last of every species. When the snow leopard's head hangs on his wall he thinks that other men will admire him, and envy what he has done."

He saw grief in her eyes, and a burning anger. "Is that why you came here – to save the snow leopard?"

"If I can," she said. "But first I must find him, before Goldbeard does."

"And then?"

"And then I'll take him to a place where not even Goldbeard can follow."

"What place is that?" asked Jang.

Instead of answering, she offered him a riddle. "The last sanctuary," she said. "The journey's end, the secret kingdom."

"Shambhala," Jang said softly, wonderingly. The name hung in the bright air – the syllables of an ancient mystery. "My grandmother said it was the country at the center of the world. She said there was no map that would take you there. You could only set your feet on the true path, and travel hopefully."

"She was right, your grandmother," Vale said.

"Let me come with you," said Jang, "to Shambhala."

Her jewel-colored eyes seemed to look clear through to his soul. She said, "Are you strong enough, I wonder? And brave enough? Not many are. Will you follow the true path, wherever it leads?"

"I will do anything, Lady. Anything."

Her mouth softened. "Perhaps you will," she said. "Come with me, then — but be warned, if you fall behind I cannot wait. And one thing more . . ."

"Yes, Lady?"

"You must promise to use no magic — no spells, no conjuring up of fires, no objects floating in the air."

He was startled. "Why not?"

"Because in these high places, the walls between the worlds are thin. There are many gateways here — not only into Shambhala, but into other places. To use magic here is to risk unlocking those doors. Do you understand?"

"Yes, Lady," he said — not understanding at all. But he gave her his promise — it seemed a small enough price to pay.

Ridge upon gray ridge fell away beneath them. At these wind-swept heights they slept in tumbledown shelters of mud and stone or in shallow caves hollowed out of the rock.

At the limits of the treeline, twisted juniper straggled up into brown alpine meadows. Beyond was a wilderness of naked tumbled rock; and then the high eternal snows, the wall at the world's edge where only gods and demons lived.

Vale stabled the pony at a mountain hamlet. "If we do not come this way again she is yours," she told the headman.

Jang was roused one morning just before dawn by the fierce howling of the snow wind. A dream still clung like tattered gauze to the edges of his mind. Vale stirred and sat up.

"Lady," he said. "I dreamt of the snow leopard."

She stared at him in the near dark.

"Where, Jang? Can you describe the place?"

He held his palms outspread. "There was snow, and shadow, and gray rock falling away below, and the sound of water. It could have been one of a thousand places."

"Go back into your dream, Jang. Go back, before it vanishes."

Jang closed his eyes, slowed his breath, let his thoughts rove free. He felt himself floating, drifting – falling into sleep as quietly as snow. As he reentered the landscape of his dream he knew he was not alone. In some strange way, Vale walked with him.

He saw a deep, snow-choked gorge with a sharp bend in it, like the crook of an arm, and a cairn of skulls, and bright red rags tied to a wind-gnarled pine. Beyond the cairn there was a choice of roads – a low one, going down into the valley bottom, and a high narrow goat track clinging to the sheer side of the ravine. On the high path he caught a glimpse of silver fur, a long, sinuous, graceful shape, a glitter of eyes like frost in moonlight.

He woke, and in the gray light met Vale's eyes. "Yes," she said. "You've dreamed well. I know the place."

Next day, as they floundered through the knee-deep drifts of the pass, Jang summoned up the courage to ask, "Are you a sorcerer, lady?"

She gave him an odd look. "Why do you ask?"

"Because last night you came with me, into my dream."

She laughed. "A simple mind skill, nothing more." What she said then made Jang look up in surprise. "If there is a danger of magic here, the danger lies with you, Jang. There is a power in you . . . unschooled, but potent. When you have such power, there are endless temptations to use it."

"But what is the harm, if I can help you to save the snow leopard?"

"The harm, Jang, is what you may unleash, in thinking to do good. In this Last Age of the World, the servants of

Darkness are stirring in their sleep, for they feel the turning of the Wheel, and know their day has come again. And remember what I said to you — that in the high places, the walls between the worlds are thin."

They came to the cairn, perched on a lip of rock, and the twisted pine with its red-rag flowers. And then, just after midday, they found a sign — the clear and unmistakable paw mark of the great white cat.

"Wait," Vale said. "The mark isn't fresh, he could be hours or days away. I must know where he is, must reach out to him."

Poised there in the high path, Vale withdrew into stillness, silence. Jang knew that at this moment Vale's spirit and the spirit of the snow leopard were somehow, inexplicably joined. And this, he thought, was not magic, not sorcery, but a natural thing, a simple and unchanging truth. For had not his hill-born grandmother taught him that all things in this world, animate and inanimate, seen and invisible, were one?

Vale opened her eyes. "I've found the snow leopard," she said softly. "And Jang, I've discovered something else — something wonderful, and unexpected. Whatever happens, we cannot let Goldbeard have her."

"A female?" he said with a small shock of surprise.

"Her mate is dead," Vale said. "Wolves killed him. But here is the thing that is so wonderful. After all, she is not the last. She's pregnant, Jang."

"How far away is she?"

"Not far. She's sheltering in one of the caves overlooking those high ledges. Somehow we must get her to the Gateway."

They climbed again, their lungs aching in the thin air. They did not see the leopard until they were nearly upon her, so well did her coat – that silken, silvery coat that was like rain-mist clouding the velvety-black rosettes – merge into the dark, ice-encrusted rock behind her. But then she looked up with her great pale eyes, as though she had been waiting for them. Rose, stretched and, moving slowly and deliberately with the weight of her unborn young, she padded down to them on her huge soft paws.

They were moving high up on a narrow rock-ledge that curved around the elbow of the gorge. The full moon, rising over the peaks, flooded the world with ghostly light. Suddenly, with a warning signal to Jang, Vale flattened herself against the cliff face.

"There it is," she whispered. "Goldbeard's camp."

Jang looked down and saw, almost directly below them, a cluster of moon-washed tents.

They inched along the ledge. Jang could feel the warm silky bulk of the leopard against him; could hear the soft snuffling of her breath. Somewhere beyond, around the curve of the ravine, was the place Vale called the Gateway. A little further now, and a wall of rock would hide them from view of the camp.

The ledge narrowed until it was no more than shoulder-width, and then it curved around a bulge of rock. There were no handholds anywhere.

"Let me go first," Vale said. She arched her body, shifted her balance, worked her way along the ledge with agonizing slowness until she found her footing on the far side of the rock bulge. Then she reached out for Jang's hand. As he strained towards her, his foot slid on a loose stone and sent it rattling down the slope. In an instant of pure terror he knew he was falling. Then he felt Vale's iron grip on his wrist, the sharp painful tug on his arm and shoulder as she wrenched him to safety. He stood gasping, where the ledge widened, with sudden cold sweat glistening on his brow.

Below, in Goldbeard's camp, someone must have heard that small rattle of a stone falling. A head thrust itself out of a tent, a voice shouted. In seconds the camp was awake. Another second, and a rifle cracked. The snow leopard's tail lashed; her eyes glittered. She tensed, sprang, a long pale shape made of frost and moonlight, and vanished into the tumble of rocks above the trail.

Jang caught a glimpse of Goldbeard, his hair and beard ice-pale above the dark leather of his coat and breeches. The moonlight glinted on the long barrel of a rifle.

"Get down," hissed Vale. Jang lay with his face pressed against cold stone, heart hammering, every muscle in his body clenched.

For the moment, something saved them – the black shadow of the cliff, the deceptiveness of moonlit distances, the hand of some watchful mountain god. But now there were a dozen men pouring out of the camp and up the scree-strewn slope towards the foot of the cliff. Jang and Vale were trapped on their high ledge, exposed and helpless. Goldbeard shouted something; Jang heard the high whine of a bullet as it struck the rock face close to his head, and the sharp crack of a rifle in the brittle air. There was no time to remember cautions, promises: there was only this blind terror scrabbling at his throat.

High up on the scarp on the opposite side of the ravine was an enormous jagged boulder, half-buried in drifting snow. Jang singled it out, instinctively, because it looked so lightly balanced that a hard push would be enough to dislodge it from its place.

In that moment of terror, he reached into himself and found an elemental, unimagined power. He became one with the rock. He could feel a shifting, a tilting, something huge and ponderous, earth-rooted, giving way. Then all at once it seemed that the whole precipice was falling – an enormous mass of rocks, ice, scree and snow, shuddering, bounding, crashing with a thunderous noise down the sheer slope into the gorge.

Afterwards there was silence. Somewhere beneath that vast expanse of moonlit rubble, beneath those tons of stone and earth and softly settling snow, Goldbeard and his camp lay buried.

There crept through the still air a high, eerie howling that lifted the hairs on Jang's neck.

"Wolves," he whispered, willing it to be true. But then Vale turned, and he saw the silvery pallor of her face in moonlight. "You have saved us, for the moment. But do you understand the cost?"

Jang said, "It was not only to save myself. It was for the snow leopard."

"What's done is done," Vale said. "Maybe there was no help for it. All the same, I fear to think what dark things your magic has loosed in this world."

She led him stumbling and sliding along the icy path, around the bend to where the way was half-choked with a litter of fallen stones.

The clouds were drifting across the moon's face. In the fitful light he caught a glimpse – no more – of a shimmering gateway; and through that gateway the wide vistas of a distant country. He saw the gleam of a river gliding among tall trees, an expanse of flowering summer meadows . . . he blinked and it was gone.

The leopard crouched on a narrow lip of rock, mouth stretched wide in a snarl of rage and terror. All around her, boiling and writhing out of the earth, came shapes of clotted shadow, malformed and hideous: wolf wraiths with eyes of flame.

Vale leaped up onto the ledge in front of the snow leopard, shielding the great cat with her body. Fangs bared, growling deep in their throats, the shadow wolves circled, their great shoulders bunched to spring.

Jang thought, *This is my doing. I have opened the doors into dark places, I have brought these monsters into the world. I have done this thing. Now I must undo it.*

He waved his arms wildly – shouting, whistling, howling; snatched up stones and ice chunks and hurled them into the midst of the pack, until the leader turned its monstrous head, the red cinders of its eyes igniting into flame; and Jang felt that terrible mindless hatred turn upon himself.

He swung on his heels, turned his back on the wolves and the shining gateway, raced like the wind itself down the icy path, careless of where his feet fell on the loose snow-powdered shale, feeling the hot breath of the demon pack behind him, hearing the dreadful soft padding of their feet.

He ran fleet-footed as a mountain sheep, swift and headlong as the river runs through the high passes. Down and down and down he ran, plunging along the steep bare slopes, over the loose scree and crusted snow and tangles of juniper scrub and sapling birch, until the dark winter forest closed around him.

He risked a quick glance over his shoulder. The pack still followed – but a strange thing was happening. Through that snarling mass of hair and flesh and bone, Jang could see, quite distinctly, the black trunks of the trees behind. As Jang led them further and ever further from the dark place that had spawned them, the demon wolves were fading, losing shape and substance, blowing away like tatters of gray mist on the wind.

Jang's steps slowed, and at last he dared to rest. Gasping, he leaned against a pine trunk, hearing only the faint sighing of the branches and the harsh pounding of his heart.

Looking up through the treetops he could see a patch of sky where a faint gray light was growing. As the light paled and the path grew plain, he went on down the mountainside to morning.

In his heart Jang knew two things: that Vale and the leopard had reached Shambhala; and that someday he would take the northward path again. In these mountains he had found a gift, or a curse, unsought, undreamed of; a power that raged in him like a black storm on the hills. He knew he must master that power, must shape it to his will, or one day it would destroy him. The gods, unasked, had given Jang magic. Wisdom was a thing he must seek out for himself.

What if . . . the animals grew huge and took over?

THE GOOD MOTHER

Priscilla Galloway

The giant clams were the real danger, but most of them would close up and bury themselves in the sand when the tide was out. It was possible to walk across to Grandma's island then, though later and earlier the cold salt ocean rushed and swirled among the rocks. The sound of the ocean was always in Ruby's ears. Sometimes it crashed, sometimes it growled, sometimes it murmured, but it was always there, defining and shaping her world. Years later, when she lived far inland, Ruby would lie sleepless night after night, missing that sound. She could never think about Grandma without her ears tingling and her nostrils prickling.

Ruby and her mum could easily walk to Grandma's house in twenty minutes. Ruby's mother carried her rifle in case of beasts, but neither of them had ever encountered one. The nearest major infestation was several hundred miles away. Woman and child did not bother to hush the sound of their footsteps on the path. Mum knew the tides. They always

clambered over the driftwood on the beach just when the
saltwater had gone out enough for them to walk across the
channel, stepping very carefully.

One day one clam was open a little, hiding under a huge
mat of green-brown seaweed. It snapped shut on the edge of
Ruby's cape. Luckily Mum had scissors in her bag. Both of
them together couldn't pull the crimson velvet loose.
Afterward Mum had to take a little tuck in the hem, but it
didn't show. Months later Ruby was still having nightmares.
"I wish Grandma had moved in with us years ago," said Mum
one night after Ruby had wakened screaming. "It would make
things so much easier now."

"Would Grandma leave her island?" Ruby was so startled
she forgot her dream, in which a giant clam had closed on
her leg above the knee. Grandma belonged in her rocking
chair in the living room of the little brown house, or nestled
in the quilts of her big carved bed.

"Don't look so shocked, child." Mum laughed wryly.
"Sometimes people do move, you know. Things do change.
But Grandma refused. 'I wouldn't be happy,' she told me, 'and
nor would you.' Maybe she was right, who knows? It's too
late now."

"Why?" asked Ruby. "Because of her heart?"

"That's right," Mum agreed. "Years ago, I might have per-
suaded her. Now I can't even try, she gets upset if she thinks
I'm hinting. She's got her oxygen, and that's a blessing, she'd
have died without it. I'm glad we didn't tell her about the
clam nearly catching you. She'd worry, and there's nothing
we can do."

Ruby never wore her precious cape again when she and
Mum went out to the island. She wore tight leggings and a
short jacket, and she and Mum watched out for clams. They

each carried a stick to poke at any of the mammoth bivalves that got in their way. The two great shells would slam closed at a touch, and then they could get around the clam easily. The creatures took a long time to open again.

They couldn't go every day, only when Mum was off duty. Even then, if there was a beast attack anywhere she could not leave. Mum's job was to relay radio messages. Often she would be passing on a frantic call for help and relaying back a message of hope. The radio would crackle as routes were described to the hunters and schedules worked out. Mum's work saved lives.

There was a beast attack the day Grandma spilled her medicine. Mum's face grew rigid as her mother's apologetic voice came through. She ripped off her headset and jumped up. Then she sat down again. "What's to be done?" she fretted. "I won't be off duty until the hunters are on the way. It could be hours. I'll miss this tide and maybe the next one too. If Grandma doesn't get more medicine, she'll die."

"I can go to Grandma's by myself. Mum, you have to let me." Ruby's round face, lifted to her mother's, was red with frustration. "I'm ten years old. I'm not a baby. I can run faster than you can. I can be careful. I can swim if I have to."

"You know you can't swim there." Mum's hand trembled on Ruby's shoulder. "That current is so fast, it'd pull you off your feet and right into a clam. I don't want to let you go by yourself. What if a beast comes whispering along? What if a clam gets you? Oh, Ruby, what can I do?"

"I'll be okay. Don't worry, Mum, nothing's going to happen." Ruby patted her mother's hand.

Her mother shivered. "Take the basket, Ruby, and get along with you. Don't stop, but don't run, just keep moving and you should get there right on low tide. Wear your rubber boots, it'll be wet walking across." *And there's a chance you could pull your foot out of the boot if a clam grabs at you*, Mum thought. "Ruby, don't forget your stick."

"Mum, I'm scared about Grandma."

"I'm scared myself, Ruby, but you should be in time. Grandma's got her oxygen. She didn't spill all her medicine. She had one dose left in the bottle, and she radioed us for help immediately. Thank goodness I've been keeping a refill on hand. I knew she'd need it some day.

"When you get there, she'll be ready for her next dose. You give it to her. You have good steady hands, you won't spill. She'll be just fine. You put on the kettle and make her a cup of tea. Be careful when you pour the hot water, Ruby."

Ruby could hear the worry in Mum's voice. "I'll be fine, Mum. I'll look after Grandma. And I won't come back tonight."

"That's right. It's much too dangerous. Clams look like rocks in the dark, and beasts might be out hunting. I'll come for you at low tide tomorrow if I can get off the radio. If I can't come myself, I'll call for help, likely get one of the hunters. It's bright sun today, that should keep you safe. The sun, and your stick."

The wicker basket bumped awkwardly against Ruby's left leg as she clumped along the path, kicking at the dry leaves, swishing her stick. The autumn sun shone warm in the brilliant unclouded sky. What child could be scared or worried on such a glorious day? Ruby ran a hundred yards or so for sheer delight. Then she dawdled, catching her breath. Walking onward, she stopped to pick wildflowers for Grandma, white Queen Anne's lace, yellow daisies, and tangled purple vetch. The tough stems bent but would not break for Ruby's chubby hands. She pulled the plants out, roots and all, adding them helter-skelter to the medicine and the bag of muffins in her basket. There was no point in hurrying. She could not go across until the tide was out.

"What are you doing, child? Does your mother know you're out?"

The gruff voice came from a dark thicket on her right. Ruby jumped, then slit her eyes, trying to see who — or what — spoke. Could the beasts really talk? Nobody ever said so, except in Grandma's stories. Ruby wished her hands were empty. "It's all right," the voice continued. "I'm a hunter. I get ready for beasts. Tell me, where do you go?"

"I'm taking Grandma her medicine across to the island. It's not dangerous. There aren't any beasts around here." Grownups were always in charge, Ruby knew. A child had to do what they said, especially a hunter. It was her or his job to keep people safe. "Mum knows I'm going," Ruby continued. "Grandma can't breathe if she doesn't get her medicine."

"Good child," the voice almost purred.

Basket and stick dropped from Ruby's hands. Her legs felt like big erasers, soft and bendy. "You're one of them, aren't you?" she whispered, not knowing why she was so sure. "You're not a hunter. You're a beast." She ran in panic into the woods, away from the purry beast voice. Then she stopped. Was it coming after her? She listened as if her life depended on it, Mum might say. Her life did depend on it. Mum had told her often enough what happened to people who got caught.

Nothing. Nothing.

Would she be able to hear it?

"One good thing about the beasts being so big," Grandma had told her, "they make a lot of noise. When Great-grandma was your age, there were lots of little creatures. Some of them were pets, but most were wild. Lots of life around then, all kinds, before the Chem Wars, and none of it could talk. Only people could talk, back then. That's how it should be. You could kill a wild mouse with a little trap and a bit of cheese. The only sound you'd hear would be the crack when the trap went off. Dirty things. I'm not sorry the mice are gone."

Ruby stopped running. She shut her mouth tight and held her nose to silence her laboring chest. There was no sound of pursuit. She let out her breath in a long sigh.

The basket! Would it still be lying on the path? Would Grandma's precious medicine be safe? Now Ruby realized she must hurry. She must get across to the island before the tide turned.

Where was the path? Had she lost her way? Ruby looked behind her. She could not see through the bushes, but she knew the path must be that way. She had pushed through bushes as she ran. Hurry, hurry, sang her pulse. No, stop and listen, urged her brain. Her blood roared in her ears. Surely the beast was there, watching the path and waiting! But then she glimpsed the basket.

Without even a second's pause Ruby darted onto the path. She grabbed the basket with both hands and turned in a circle, all in the same motion. Nothing. The danger had gone away. Now she ran. Her side hurt. Her feet slipped inside the loose rubber boots. She could feel her socks bunching. How much farther?

Crashing, growling, the ocean pounded before her. Her nostrils prickled with the dank smell of kelp. Then she was into coarse sand, feet and boots slipping, almost tripping among the rocks. Her stick must still be where she had dropped it when she ran from the beast. The tide was turning. Eddies tugged at her boots. Little waves swirled. Ruby fell once, but did not lose her grip on the precious basket. Several clams were out and open a little, waiting. Ruby managed to get around them easily enough. Once she poked a flower at a monster that filled the gap between two big rocks. It snapped shut. Ruby shivered as she climbed over it.

Nearing the other side at last, she pushed the basket onto a dark shelf of rock and scrambled up, scraping both legs. Ouch! Barnacles! Holes opened up in her tights; the white exposed skin turned bright red immediately as blood spurted from the razor-sharp cuts. It didn't hurt, not yet, though she knew it would hurt a lot later. Any other time, Ruby would have been crying for a bandage and a hug. Now she was merely thankful. The nightmare was almost over. Up the path through the trees she could already glimpse the cedar shakes of Grandma's cottage.

Ruby bent to pick up her basket. But what was that mark in the sand? She moved the basket aside. Could it be a paw print? It was almost as big around as the basket. The afternoon sky had clouded over. Soon the air would begin to cool. The dangerous dark would arrive. Ruby shivered and ran across the beach and up the path to Grandma's door.

Meanwhile, at the cottage, Grandma kept going to the door and opening it, looking for Ruby. Any other time she would have kept her home locked and barred. But her daughter had radioed to tell her Ruby was coming with the medicine. "The child!" Grandma had been horrified. "What if a clam gets her?" she screamed. "Or a beast? I'd rather take my chances without my medicine. It's no favor to me if Ruby gets hurt."

"Too late now." Mum had sounded very tired. "Relax, Mum, can't you? She's on her way."

So Grandma threw open her door as soon as she heard the knock. "You're here, Ruby," she cried. "Thank goodness you're safe, child. Come in, come in."

But Ruby did not come in.

Grandma peered into the outdoors. Her eyes saw — but her mind refused. Not furry legs! No, no. Not a long beast snout! No. In a merciful faint, Grandma dropped to the floor.

The beast squeezed her monstrous body through the narrow door with some difficulty. Once inside she tried to stand upright and banged her head. On all fours, however, she had ample room. The beast stared thoughtfully down at Grandma's body. Should she take it now to her hungry cubs? Her children would want it alive. They would want flowing blood to lick, and she would want twitching flesh to tear and chew. But the other one would come soon. More flesh, more blood.

The smoothskins are so small, the great beast thought. *It'll take the two of them to make a decent meal.* Food was getting harder and harder to find. Dimly the beast remembered earlier times, when almost any flesh had sufficed except that of her own kind. These days, fur, feather, fin made common cause against the smoothskins. The great beast would take other meat for her babies only if she had no choice.

She pulled the limp body of her catch along the floor and dumped it on the far side, between the low bed and the wall, where she could swat it down easily if need arose. The other smoothskin could run fast. How could she get it to come close enough to grab?

With her great paw she swatted at the big overhead light, only to leap back with a scream as pain jolted through her body. Trembling and weak, she climbed onto the bed and pulled the coverings over her hairy, furry self. If she lay sideways and bent her four strong legs, she could fit, though only just. The glare of light was gone; now she could see.

At once the creature saw the face beside the bed! She threw herself at it, landing in a tangle of claws and covers, the face crumpling under her. On the other side of the face was a long tube. The beast held the face tentatively to her own snout. She pulled the string attached to the face. The string jumped back against the face and hurt her other paw. Yes, she could put the face over her snout and pull the stretchy string over her head. The long tube went to a silver cylinder beside the bed. It smelled all wrong. It hurt to breathe. She tore off the face. Just the same, she would use the face when the little smoothskin came. It was the right size and shape for a smoothskin. It was not the right shape for a beast – too long and not enough snout – and what snout there was, was in the wrong place. But it would help trick the little smoothskin. Yes, she would certainly do that.

"Mother. Come in, Mother. Has Ruby got there yet? Come in."

The creature, still tangled in quilts and face, whirled around again.

The voice was coming from a box on top of a table. The creature whipped the chair aside with one paw and nuzzled the box. What could this be?

"Mother. Are you all right, Mother? Come in. Come in."

Was this smoothskin inside the box? With one swipe the creature sent it flying. It crashed noisily to the floor. Buttons and knobs flew; sharp, gleaming shards fell out. The creature very cautiously picked up one long, bright sliver. Now she held the sliver against her own hairy epidermis. Ouch! Bright blood! She dropped the sliver and licked at her blood automatically. Then she bent and picked the gleaming, sharp thing up again. She might take it to her den. With it she could open the smoothskins' blood right over her babies' open mouths.

Rat-a-tat! Such a light tapping on the door! "Grandma! I'm here!" Such a little voice! A strange warmth tugged at the huge creature inside the cottage, akin somehow to the fierce love she felt for her own little ones. Her confused feelings, however, did not slow her responses. In one leap she gained the bed and fell on it, gathering the quilts about her as best she could. She reached for the face, ready to slip the stretchy cord around her head.

"Come in, dear," she called. Her voice sounded quivery to her own ears, echoing her shakiness. "It's not locked."

The door flew open and banged shut. Ruby threw the bolt before rushing over to the bed. "Here's your medicine, Grandma," she panted. "I ran as fast as I could. Oh, Grandma," – the light voice quivered – "you needed your oxygen mask. I was too slow." The creature was totally still under the face and the quilts. "I'll just turn on the light," Ruby went on. "Then I can see to measure out your medicine. Ouch! This kettle is boiling. I guess you're ready for your tea."

Ruby's feet crunched on glass as she went to the light switch. Now that her eyes were getting used to the dim light, she could see the wreckage of the radio. Now she looked with new eyes at the bed, hearing again in her mind the purry voice from the woods. That mound on the bed was too big! Terror coursed through every vein. Ruby's mind blanked.

The covers moved a little. In horrid fascination Ruby watched. She glimpsed a vast paw, saw the dark triangle of a huge ear above the concealing mask. For a long moment, girl and beast were still.

Then the creature moved again. With a scream Ruby grabbed the big kettle and threw it, not noticing her own burned hands. Those hands threw back the bolt and opened the door in a single motion. Ruby ran uphill behind the cottage into the trees. No conscious thought was involved, but her feet headed away from the beach, where the current

now boiled and surged. There would be no escape before the
next low tide. Ruby was almost at the other end of the island
before the pain in her side forced her to stop. She fell onto a
mossy rock and sat, willing her laboring breath to quiet, listening for the beast.

Now she actually heard the sea sounds, the rhythmic
crash of waves and the constant undertone of the immense
ocean, the waters moving ceaselessly. As her ears adjusted,
she began to distinguish the land sounds – cracks, rustles,
birdcalls. Ruby cowered. As the minutes passed and nothing
happened, the child's mind began to function again.

Grandma was dead. She must be dead.

What now? A cave? A tree? Anything was better than
waiting for the creature to come. Then Ruby remembered
her very own cave. She was sure it had once been a smugglers' cave, though she had found no gold or jewels; no liquor
either, only three tall brown bottles against the back wall.
"Beer bottles," Grandma had laughed. "Old ones, but lots of
people used to drink beer like that. I did myself when I was
young. We can pretend it was smugglers, can't we?"

Ruby's eyes stung. As she caught her breath, she was
beginning to realize that she would never joke and laugh
with Grandma again. Although she had not been to the cave
for at least a year, she knew exactly where it was. In the
fading light she clambered down over the boulders and
around the prickly gorse to reach its entrance, not far above
the surging waves.

What had changed? The entrance – it was bigger. Surely
those two rocks had almost closed it off. Maybe not, it had
been a long time. Ruby slipped inside. She always had to feel
her way toward the shelf near the back. Long ago Grandma
had given her a candle in a bright red candleholder and

matches in a waterproof canister. "You can leave them in your cave," Grandma said. "These days, nobody else goes there. You can play smugglers and show a light for your pals."

Had her eyes adjusted more quickly, or was there really more light? Hard to be sure. But the smell! Her cave had never smelled like this: sharp, pungent. Again Ruby stopped. Her eyes darted about the cave. What was that? Something . . . not very large. Her hands closed on the candle and matches. In the flickering light she sighed deeply; some of the tension began to pass.

Now Ruby could see what was making the smell. She knelt in wonder. Her free hand went gently toward one of the minuscule bodies. It stirred a little. A tiny mouth opened and made slurping, sucking noises. Then it closed again. The baby slept on. Ruby knew they were babies, but she had never seen babies like these. Four of them, and all four could have fitted easily into the basket she had carried to Grandma's house earlier that afternoon, so long ago.

"We had lots of pets when I was a child." Grandma could go on for hours talking about her terrier Samantha. "It was a big joke in our family. I named the dog Sam. What a surprise when Sam had puppies! My mother helped me find a better name. Ruby, Sam's two puppies were so tiny they could fit in my hand, both at the same time!" The big family album held several photos of little-girl Grandma wheeling the puppies in her doll carriage. The color had faded, but those little creatures looked very much like the four in front of Ruby now in the cave.

Ruby could hardly breathe. "I've wanted a pet forever," she whispered. "Please, little doggies, let one of you be mine."

On cue, one of the babies opened its sleepy eyes. Ruby put down the candle. Then she slid a hand under the tiny body and held its warmth, stroking and murmuring. This was better than her velvet cape! Again she remembered Grandma's words: "You'll never have a puppy, darling. All the dogs have died."

Could Grandma have been wrong? Whose babies could these be?

As she asked herself, Ruby knew. No wonder the cave entrance seemed bigger. She had run from Grandma's house right to the home of the beast!

Ruby ran from the cave without stopping to put down the baby or blow out the candle. At this end of the island there was no beach. The child looked over a small, rocky cliff to breakers that crashed against the rocks below. The day was darkening.

"I have to throw this little beast over the cliff into the waves," Ruby told herself. "I have to. Then I have to go back and get the others and throw them over too. I have to. They'll grow up and kill people. Their mother killed Grandma."

She hugged the warm little body tighter. The creature gave a startled yelp. "It's okay," sang Ruby, stroking it again. The little mouth found her finger. Noisily the baby began to suck. "You're hungry," said Ruby. "I haven't got any food. Poor little thing." She turned her back on the cliff and the waves and walked again toward Grandma's house. Perhaps she could put down the baby for the beast to pick up. Perhaps the beast would forget about her and look after its young.

By this time the beast was indeed intent on returning to her cubs with her one smoothskin. The kettleful of boiling water had burned her in spite of her fur, and she was still feeling shaky from the electric shock.

Grandma, on the other hand, was regaining her energy. Earlier she had started to come round and had managed to get the oxygen mask over her face without being noticed.

Now, on her knees on the far side of the bed, she saw Ruby's basket lying in the broken glass on the floor. "Ruby, where are you?" she cried.

"The little smoothskin? She ran away," replied the beast. "I'll get her later. My babies and I need both of you."

"The stories are true, then. You can talk. I never believed it, not really."

"Believe what you like," said the beast indifferently. "You'll be just as good one way or the other."

"Good for what? What do you need us for?"

"Food, of course." The beast sounded impatient.

"I need my medicine." The beast watched casually while Grandma plodded over to the basket. As she bent for the life-giving liquid, she glanced under her bed, checking the position of her old rifle. It had not been cleaned for months (everybody knew there were no beasts hereabouts), but it was loaded.

"I feel sick." The old woman lumbered back to the bed and fell on it. Her right hand reached down and closed on the stock of the gun. She swung it up fast, cocked, and fired. By the time the gun had gone off, the beast was on her and had seized it. The two great hairy forelegs bent the gun as if it had been a stick of eraser and tossed the debris out the door. "This fire stick killed my sister. This fire stick killed my mother." A flash of claws swept over Grandma's face, almost touching, almost slashing, but not quite.

I've still got the little revolver, Grandma thought. The tiny ivory-handled weapon was in the desk. In her head Grandma fired at the beast's head, at its belly, at the thickset neck. It would scarcely matter. She was no great pistol shot. The tiny bullets were meant to threaten a burglar, a human invader of times gone by. Like as not she'd miss completely. Even if her aim was good, a bit of lead might hurt the great beast but would hardly slow it down. Grandma looked at the clock. Six hours still to pass before the hunters could get across.

Why was she so sure that anybody would come?

Logic confirmed her intuition. The radio lay smashed on the floor. Her daughter would call and call and get no response. That would be enough. Now Ruby's mother would be getting frantic. Soon she would summon help. The hunters would have some distance to travel, but they could not get across until slack tide. Grandma had to force a delay.

Easy. Let the exhaustion in. Grandma let her muscles go limp. Let the beast see that the loss of the rifle had finished her. She closed her eyes.

The mask was suddenly pushed onto her face, the oxygen hissing. Grandma's faded blue eyes opened to the soft brown eyes of the beast. Its breath warmed her face; its pungent smell mixed with the oxygen in her nose.

"We must go soon," said the beast. "We must feed my cubs."

Grandma visualized her blood flowing, little creatures sucking.

"I'm tired," she sighed. "Wait a little."

The beast crouched. "This is not a good place," she said. "There is no food and it is difficult to come and go." How could she safely move her tiny cubs? She could carry only one at a time, in her mouth. She would have to go quickly on the next tide. Other fire sticks would come.

"We go now," she ordered. "You go first."

"I must open the window," said Grandma. The casement flew open at her touch as the beast's paw pushed her outside. While the gigantic creature struggled through the door, Grandma reached through the window and swung back the top of the desk. One swift motion and the little pistol was in her hands. There was no time to aim; she pointed and fired even as the huge paw swatted her to the ground.

At the side of the cottage, Ruby screamed. Her hands tightened convulsively; the cub squealed. The beast stood on three legs, the left forepaw raised, held protectively to its body, eyes fixed on cub and child. Grandma sat up slowly, her left arm dangling at an odd angle. Almost casually she tried to put it where it belonged; then the pain hit. She leaned weakly against the cottage.

Keeping her distance, Ruby walked forward until she was even with the front of the cottage. Now they could all see each other. Without speaking, Ruby began to edge her way backward down the slope that led to the sea.

"Stop," cried the beast. "Bring my baby." Her eyes darted to Grandma, then back to her child.

"No!" screamed Ruby. She turned and ran for the rocky, barnacled shelf she had climbed before. Below, the water swirled and rushed; waves crashed with their uneven repeated rhythm. Ruby held the baby away from her body. She turned sideways, watching but poised to whirl and throw the tiny beast.

The scene was frozen: Ruby with arms outstretched at the ocean's edge, the three-legged beast above her on the path, Grandma like a broken doll against the cottage. The beast baby squealed and wailed.

"Bring it to me," entreated the beast. "See, I have blood." She lowered her paw. Ruby could see blood against the dark, hairy coat.

"Grandma," cried Ruby. "It's so little, Grandma. What should I do?"

"Make her move for it," called Grandma. "Put it down

where you are, Ruby, and come up to me. Keep away from both of them."

Ruby had to force her body to obey. She had to make her back bend down, force her arms to lower the little creature to the soft moss, will her fingers to open and let go. Then she could move to Grandma, while the beast lumbered to her cub.

Time passed. Beast lay quiescent; cub drank and cuddled. Ruby tried and failed to pull Grandma's dislocated shoulder back in place. She carried blankets, painkillers, medicine, oxygen to her grandmother, then sat beside her. Time passed.

The beast was the first to rouse. "My other babies," she muttered. "I need them. They need food. I have food, but I cannot get to them. Too weak."

Ruby thought about the other little creatures. Tears gathered in her eyes. "Oh, Grandma, what should I do?"

Grandma considered. "Go and get them," she said at last. "Take the basket to put them in. I'll think about what to do when you get back."

But when Ruby got back with the basket full of wailing, naked little creatures, she could only run and hand them to their mother. "Grandma, they're so hungry," she gasped, and Grandma nodded as she ran by.

Blood still oozed from the tiny bullet hole above the beast's left paw, but very slowly. "Squeeze me," ordered the beast, "make blood come." Ruby's lungs were filled with the smell of beast as she massaged the hairy hide around the hole with both hands, urging out the blood, while in turn the mother held her little ones to drink.

The fourth cub opened sleepy eyes on Ruby, who picked it up and cuddled it again. Leaving the beast with the other three, she went back to Grandma. "It's a problem of food, as I see it," Grandma said slowly. "They can reason; they can talk; they have feelings. Food. That's the problem."

"Yes, Grandma," Ruby agreed.

"Babies used to have milk," said Grandma. "Milk from their mothers, or milk from cows, or milk from soybeans, it didn't matter. She hasn't got any milk for them, that's for sure. There haven't been any cows since I was your age, Ruby. But I've got soybean milk. Think I've even got a baby bottle. Climb up to the cupboard above the fridge, Ruby; use the step stool. Fill the bottle and heat it for twenty seconds in the microwave. Can you do all that?" Grandma's voice was tender. Ruby returned her smile as she pushed open the door.

In a moment she was back, hurrying to the beast and the three still-hungry babies. "Food," said Ruby, in response to the beast's raised paw. The paw lowered, and Ruby picked up a little wailing body. In a moment the baby was sucking noisily. Ruby laid baby and bottle along the mother's vast forearm.

"Help me, Ruby," called Grandma. "I want to get down the slope there with the rest of you." Both faces were white and sweaty by the time Grandma was settled again.

"Here, take them." The beast handed another baby and the half-full bottle to Ruby. "Show me where it goes." She pointed to Grandma's dangling arm. Grandma nodded. Amazing that the huge paws could be so delicate! The paw on the beast's injured side braced Grandma while the other paw pulled and twisted. The shoulder was in again. Grandma's head lolled back against the beast. "Get the face for her," ordered the beast.

Ruby ran for the oxygen. For a while everything was in a muddle. Then Grandma was breathing well again and starting to get back some color. Ruby got another bottle of warm soy milk, and the last of the babies was fed. The beast's wound had stopped bleeding.

They hardly noticed how dark it had got. The tide would be on the ebb.

Grandma spoke at last. "You need food. We need protection against the clams. If you can tear them loose and bring them ashore, I can kill them. Is their flesh good food for you?"

"Likely," replied the beast. "If I am careful, I can tear a clam out of the sea and bring it onto land, but then it will not open, not until it has died, and the flesh has died and it is not good anymore."

"Can you manage to come down closer to the shore?" asked Grandma. "Let's see what we can do."

"How kill them?"

"The old clambake barrel," said Grandma. "It held enough clams for a hundred people. Or the sap kettle. Haven't used either one of them in forty years! We'll build a fire under the barrel and fill it with water. Drop a clam in and it will open and die. The little ones did. Don't see why the big ones would be any different."

"All right," agreed the beast. "We will go to the shore."

In the moonlight the three stared down. The channel was almost bare again. They could all see one of the giant clams, open a little, waiting greedily. Grandma reached down with a long stick. The clamshells thudded closed. Lightly the beast bounded to the ocean floor. Out came the great talons; the right paw swung beneath the clam.

Bang!

The beast was hurled backward. Into the opening between creature and clam Ruby leapt. "Stop shooting, you hunters," cried Grandma. "I knew you'd be here, and I forgot. Stop shooting now. Careful, child, crouch down," she called to Ruby, who was standing as best she could in front of the great beast.

Another shot rang out. Ruby fell back. "Stop it!" Grandma was screaming now. The shooting stopped.

Ruby was not afraid. Grandma would make the hunters help her and the beast. The girl lay against the hairy creature, breathing its pungent smell. It wrapped a huge paw around her, holding her warmly, putting pressure on her slim white arm where blood was spurting. Above the steady pulse of the ocean, another steady beat filled the child's ears: the beast's own strongly beating heart. Ruby looked up. From this angle, the creature's eyes and ears weren't big at all.

Nor were its teeth.

What if . . . a boy becomes the evil mask he tries on?

THE MASK

Joan Clark

Louie's face came into view. Stephen saw an outstretched hand. He grabbed the hand and it pulled him into the cave.

The weight of dead air pressed against Stephen's chest. He coughed. "I can't see a thing in here. You got any matches?"

Louie dug a match out of his pocket and struck it against a rock. Immediately the flame flared up, and he saw pictures on the wall.

"Look at these," he said. His voice bounced off the walls of the cave and came back to him, making him feel insignificant.

The pictures were faint. There were smudges of red, faded like blood stains and dark lines deeply incised into the rock. By following the lines the boys deciphered the shapes of strange creatures, half-man, half-beast, dressed in skins. One had the antlered head of a stag, another the head of a bear. Both had sharp claws for hands. Still another had a human face but coyote's ears.

"The first masks," Stephen murmured, and the match went out.

"They look like medicine men to me," Louie spoke into the dark. He shivered and lit another match.

It was true. The creatures were holding bone rattles and furred sticks.

"They must go back to the Ice Age," Louie said. He followed the pictures along the rough wall. He felt better having something to hold onto, a thread that wove back through time. Louie's foot hit a hollow rounded object. He lit another match and looked down.

A human skull leered up at him. He dropped the match. In its wavering light he caught a glimpse of other bones spread across the cave floor. The match went out.

"I have only one match left," he said.

Stephen's foot kicked another skull, smaller than the first. It clattered down a slight incline towards the back of the cave.

"I wonder if the Wild Man of the Woods is here," he whispered.

Lightning flashed in the mouth of the cave. In its blinding light Stephen saw a greenish-black mask on a rock shelf in front of him. Above a hooked nose that crooked under itself, two eyes caught fire. They glowed redly. Stephen felt two eyeholes drill into his chest. He fell forward onto his knees and looked up at the mask. There was a rumble of thunder. Two rows of shark's teeth grated against each other. Stephen felt as if his bones were being ground into a fine powder. There was a clacking noise cold as icicles.

Stephen saw a hand touch the tangled hair. But before Louie could pick up the mask, Stephen reached up, grabbed the face and slipped it over his. Then he stood up.

"I am the Wild Man of the Woods," he bellowed.

Lightning flashed; for an instant the cave was filled with sulfurous light.

"That'll give those bullies Willard and Sludge a big scare," Louie said admiringly, but his voice shook.

The inside of the mask smelt musty. There was a layer of something powdery lining it that clung to Stephen's skin. "I am the Wendigo," he roared.

Thunder rumbled.

Stephen staggered forward under the weight of the mask.

Instinctively Louie backed up towards the cave entrance. He tripped over a skull.

"C'mon, Steve," he said. "Take that thing off. We only want to use it to scare Willard and Sludge."

But Stephen had no intention of taking it off. He liked wearing the mask. It gave him a feeling of immense power. He felt he could beat up anyone who crossed his path. He could knock the heads off not only Willard and Sludge but anyone who'd ever bullied him.

"You know Angus told us it was dangerous," Louie said. His voice was trembling. "Take off that mask!"

"What mask?" the voice rumbled. Stephen was beginning to feel that the Wild Man of the Woods was not a mask, that it had become his head, that *he* was the Wild Man of the Woods. His head no longer felt too heavy for the rest of his body.

"Take it off!" Louie reached for the mask.

Wild Man pushed the hand roughly aside.

"You heard me!" Louie's voice quavered.

Wild Man gave him a shove. This boy was beginning to make him angry. Wild Man drilled him with his red eyes.

Red is the fire, the fight, the fight, he chanted.

Louie groped for his wooden spear and whacked it against the mask, trying to knock it off. But Wild Man deflected the blow with his sword. He knocked Louie to the cave floor, grabbed the end of the rope they had brought, and tied it around Louie's wrists and ankles. Then he ground his teeth together with satisfaction. This boy was being a pest, yammering at him to take off a mask. But he had fixed him. Wild Man wanted no one to get in his way. He would break out of this cave. He would avenge the bullies of this world and no one, least of all this puny-fleshed boy, was going to stop him.

"Aw c'mon, Steve," Louie said. "You're carrying this too far."

Shut your face, Wild Man growled. Already he had forgotten Louie's name. He picked up the homemade sword and shield and left the cave. He did not bother using the rope but crossed the narrow path in superhuman strides. As he went he chanted,

> *Break away the night, the night*
> *Tear away the flesh*
> *Red is the fire, the fight, the fight*
> *My thirst for blood is black.*

From inside the cave Louie heard the voice mumbling its horrible chant. It didn't sound like Steve. In fact the person inside the mask didn't seem to *be* Steve: it was someone else. Steve wasn't the sort of person to knock down a friend and tie him up for no reason. It was as if he'd gone wild, completely out of control. Louie heard rocks sliding; he held his breath. Steve had used the rope to tie him up instead of to help get himself safely across the slope. What if his cousin fell down the mountain side? He wouldn't stop until he reached the bottom where the stream ran. By then he'd be dead. But Steve didn't fall. Louie heard him on the other side of the slope slamming his sword against a tree, chanting those strange words. Louie slowly let out his breath. Now that his cousin had made it across he had better see to his own safety. He had to get out of this creepy cave.

Fortunately the rope had been carelessly knotted. He wriggled his hands out of their loops without too much trouble. Then he untied his ankles. Holding onto the rope and carrying his spear, he got himself across the slope. He glanced up at the sky. The clouds were ominously low. Behind them he heard the rumble of thunder. A drop of rain splattered his cheek. He'd have to find Steve. See if he couldn't knock that terrifying mask off his head before he got himself into trouble.

Instead of following the rock wall, his cousin had gone through the brush, leaving a trail of broken bushes in his wake. Louie followed this crooked trail at a safe distance. He wanted the advantage of seeing Steve before Steve saw him. The trail continued until the fire tree. Crouched behind a protective screen of leaves, Louie watched his cousin. Steve was hacking at the charred pole with a jackknife. It was *his* jackknife, Louie thought, the one Steve had given him as a present. He must have taken it from the knapsack. What a strange thing to be doing with it. Steve had completely flipped his lid, gone wacko. As Steve gouged and hacked at the tree, Louie heard him chant,

> *Break away the night, the night*
> *Tear away the flesh*
> *Red is the fire, the fight, the fight*
> *My thirst for blood is black.*

The evil head wobbled from side to side, keeping an unsteady rhythm.

Hearing this dreadful chant made Louie angry with himself and with Steve. Why had they been so foolish to think they could use an evil mask to get even with Willard and Sludge? Getting even no longer seemed important. The more he watched the mask wobble from side to side, the more convinced Louie became that he'd better not try to knock it off; at least, he had better not try it alone. Steve was armed with a sword and a jackknife. If Louie failed to get the mask off, his cousin might turn on him again. Steve seemed a lot bigger now that he was the Wild Man of the Woods. He might tie Louie to the black tree, tighter this time, and go off and leave him here. Then Louie'd be unable to get help.

Abruptly the Wild Man of the Woods broke off his chant as if he could hear Louie's thoughts. His head swiveled so that the two red eyes burned through the leaves. Louie ducked down and willed himself into stone so that shaking leaves wouldn't give him away. Terror tripled the seconds racing with the loudness of his heart. The red eyes drilled through the leaves around Louie.

Louie smelled something burning. After what seemed a very long time, the head swiveled back to the pole and the chant resumed. Louie stood up. The leaves where he'd been standing were singed brown. He crouched down again and crawled with painstaking slowness through the bushes.

Once he heard a crashing in the woods behind him. He whirled, expecting to see the Wild Man of the Woods lunge at him, but it was only a surprised deer retreating at the sound of his advance. On he went until he came to the plateau. From there he caught a glimpse of the gray lake. He heard the sound of a motorboat, felt rain on his cheek.

Behind him he heard something crash through the trees. There was a loud mumbling. The Wild Man of the Woods was coming. Louie slid down the rocky slope, stroked

quickly through the sea of willows, ducked under the
sentinel firs. He looked over the stormy lake. Far out he saw
Angus's green canoe. He caught sight of *The Explorer's* red
nose in the green grass.

He had started towards the dory when a motorboat surged
out of the reeds. In it were Sludge and Willard. The mumbling behind him became louder. There was a sharp crack of
wood against wood as Wild Man lopped a branch from a sentinel fir. Fearfully Louie looked over his shoulder and saw the
monster mask appear from beneath the sentinel firs. It was
coming straight for him.

> *Red is the fire, the fight, the fight*
> *My thirst for blood is black.*

There was no time to get into *The Explorer*. Louie threw
down the knapsack and, spear in hand, leaped into the gray
water.

The Wild Man of the Woods stood on the shore of the
lake. Thunder reverberated inside his head. Wind blew the
snaky hair across his face. Red eyes pierced the fuzzy gloom.
They picked out the blurred form of someone far away pad-
dling a green canoe. Closer to shore the eyes drilled into
three boys in a motorboat. They looked vaguely familiar.
One of the boys was fat, another thin. Bullies. They were the
bullies he was after. He wanted to bash in their skulls. Wild
Man peered at the third boy. He knew him better. He was
the one he'd tied up in the cave, the one who had tried to
knock off his head. He had escaped and now he had joined
those bullies. This made Wild Man's bile rise hot in his
mouth: he ground his teeth, slavering for revenge. *Tear away
the flesh*, he rumbled. That boy had double-crossed him,
which meant he was an enemy too.

Fight! Wild Man roared at the boys in the boat. He charged forward, then remembered that there was something between him and that boat. Water. Wild Man did not like water. His head turned from side to side, looking for a way to avoid touching the water and still reach those boys in the boat. His eyes lasered onto something bright red in the green grass.

He started towards the dory, swinging his sword back and forth as he went, whacking it against anything that grew in his path: trees, bushes, grass.

> *Break away the night, the night*
> *Tear away the flesh.*

He got into *The Explorer*, threw down his sword and shield, picked up the oars and began to row, his powerful shoulders stroking rhythmically with the chant. As he came closer to the motorboat he was pleasantly aware of helpless gestures and bulging eyes. He heard a babble of frightened voices.

"Start the motor, Sludge!"

"I can't! It's flooded."

"He's nearly here. Paddle!"

"I got nothing to paddle *with*!"

"Use your hands, then."

There was a helpless thrashing of water.

"Keep on, keep on. I'll try to hold him off with my spear." The voice belonged to the double-crosser. Wild Man rowed towards him.

"Try the motor again!"

The motorboat rocked as a bulky weight shifted itself. Water sloshed over the bow.

"Watch it! You'll have us all overboard."

Wild Man had reached the floundering boat. He looked up into the hostile, terrified eyes of a young boy. Up rose a pale arm, white as a skull-bone. It was holding a spear.

Red is the blood, the fight, the fight.

Wild Man's tongue lolled between his red lips. He grated his teeth together. He bashed his sword against the spear. The spear broke in two. One half went in the water.

Thunder rolled up the valley. It was as if the mountain dinosaurs had wakened from their prehistoric slumber, transformed into fiery dragons ready for battle. Lightning fractured the sky in bone-sharp breaks. Clouds bulged low like swollen veins.

Rain splattered on Louie's head. It felt like a heavy wet blanket flapping in his face, suffocating him. Through the murky air he watched Wild Man lift his sword again.

"Paddle harder!" he screamed to the others. Willard and Sludge flailed the water with their hands. The boat jerked forward in feeble spurts.

One pull on the oars and Wild Man had caught up with them again. He dropped the oars and began thrashing the sword about in the air, his head wobbling unsteadily. For a moment Louie thought there was enough of Steve inside that terrible mask for him to recognize his cousin. Louie reached out and grabbed hold of the wooden sword blade, trying to push it into the water. He cut himself. Blood spurted across his palm. He heard the mask mouth mumble, a strange jumble of words:

Flesh . . . red . . . thirst.

Louie kept wrestling with the question of how much of his cousin was inside this creature. The creature stood up. He lifted his warrior shield and swung the sword over his ugly head.

Louie balanced what was left of his spear on his shoulder and hesitated. He wanted to destroy this evil creature, to strike it through the heart, but he still believed his cousin Steve was in that body somewhere.

Louie couldn't do it. What he did instead was to bring the spear hard against the creature's head. Wild Man of the Woods lost his balance and toppled into the lake.

The lake sizzled from the impact. There was the snarl of iron as if a blacksmith's fiery hammer had been plunged into ice water. The lake went from gray to black. It foamed and bubbled, swirled into a whirlpool. The mask didn't sink immediately. It spun in a slow circle, its mouth open, red bubbling from between shark teeth, eyes staring into the eye of the storm. There was a crash of thunder. A lightning bolt struck the whirlpool, splitting the mask in half, and it sank. The lake surface heaved and broke. Then gradually the black faded into gray.

"Hooray!" Willard and Sludge clapped their hands. "Got him!"

"Shut up, you dummies," Louie said. "You only know the half of it. My cousin's disappeared."

Louie searched the water. There was no sign of Steve. It was as if the lake had suddenly opened up and swallowed him into a deep chasm. On top of the water floated a shield, a sword and two halves of a spear.

Louie felt sick and hollow inside. Behind him Sludge and Willard lapsed into a sulky silence. Louie felt like telling them his cousin's disappearance was all their fault. *They* had *started* this war. If they hadn't been so mean, he and Steve wouldn't have been driven to getting that evil mask out of the cave and using it for revenge.

But as he sat there in tears of anger and despair, the rain falling around him, Louie knew this wasn't the whole truth. The whole truth had to include the fact that somewhere during the fighting he should have said, Stop, we won't play this game any more. Getting even had only kept the war alive. At the time he had enjoyed it. The truthfulness of this knowledge made Louie feel worse. Through the murky air he heard the clear note of a bell. His parents were ringing for him to come home. Home was just across the lake, but it might have been in another galaxy, Louie thought. And the rain fell harder.

Stephen was several feet underwater. The blow of the mask hitting the water had stunned him. All he remembered was seeing Louie sitting in a boat with Sludge and Willard and brandishing a spear. Stephen couldn't bear to remember the look on Louie's face: it was a look of dislike and fear. Stephen sank deeper, swallowing water. He wanted the picture of Louie's hostile face to go away. It was the face of an enemy, not a friend. This confused him. It made him wonder if everyone in the world was his enemy. A feeling of intense loneliness swept over him. He sank deeper, drowning in blackness.

Then he felt himself being lifted up out of the water. And like a limp fish he was hauled into Angus's green canoe.

Later, recovering in bed, he reread the book about Masks. *Give a man a mask and he will tell the truth*, it said. He wondered what that meant, what the truth was. Could wearing a mask make you tell the truth about yourself, things like violence and revenge that you'd rather hide in nightmares? Was the truth that meanness wasn't just in the faces of other people, but in your own as well, where you couldn't see it?

"I wonder," Louie said still later. "If we put people into outer space will we carry war out there too?" He added, "Like garbage?"

"There must be some place that isn't contaminated," Stephen said. He meant a place that was perfect – for him, peace was more than an absence of war.

"Maybe it's here," Louie said. "If we can find it."

What if . . . you found a magic scepter?

THE STONE SCEPTER

Edo van Belkom

Aidan Caine stepped cautiously between the puddles and mud patches the flood had left behind. He'd been scavenging the plain all morning for things the flood had brought down from the villages upriver, but so far all he'd found was a horseshoe, two buttons, a belt buckle, and a tin cup.

The horseshoe and the tin cup could be traded for a meal at the inn, but the buttons and buckle . . . well, maybe he'd polish them up till they shone, and then sew them on his coat. Yes, when people saw those glittering buttons they'd know right off that he was no grubby son of a shoemaker, but a special boy who could make things sparkle; a boy who had the power to turn dirty old buttons into bits of glittery gold.

He took one of the buttons from his pocket and rubbed it against his palm. It was dented and bent, and the dragon's-head design on the front of it was scratched and pitted. Aidan gave it a last rub and sighed. Even a goldsmith couldn't restore its luster. Perhaps it could be melted down and made into a new button, but there was nothing magical about that. Nothing at all.

Aidan resumed his search of the plain. Most of the large and useful items like chairs and bowls and doors had already been claimed by search parties sent down from the villages. There were still things scattered about, but only those that could be easily replaced. After all, people just didn't have the time to look for buttons in the mud when there were villages to rebuild and rumors of dragon attacks to the north. The thought of that made Aidan tremble with a mix of fear and excitement. Dragons were magical beasts and he loved all things magical.

After several minutes hunched over the ground, Aidan stood up, placed his hands on his hips, and arched his aching back. Another hour or so and he'd return to the village to barter for his supper. Just thinking about it made his stomach growl. Maybe less than an hour.

He rubbed his fists into his tired eyes and, when he opened them, he noticed something strange jutting out from an odd-shaped puddle. The puddle extended out in different directions like the fingers of a hand, and rising from the middle of it was a gnarled piece of wood. It was rough and scarred, but seemed to be the perfect shape for a walking stick, the kind wizards and mages favored.

Aidan stepped forward and began wading into the puddle. When he reached the walking stick, he wrapped his hands around it tightly so he'd have a firm grip when he tried to remove it from the ground. He set his feet, counted to three and pulled . . .

The stick came away with ease, sending Aidan falling backwards into another puddle. Gasping for breath, he wiped the dirty water from his face with his left hand and looked at the stick in his right. The surface of it was hard, not like wood at all. It was more like stone, but very light, unlike any type of rock he knew.

Aidan jabbed the walking stick into the ground and used it to help himself up. When he got to his feet he realized the stick was longer than he'd first thought. It reached above his waist almost to his chest, making it look more like a scepter than a simple stick.

Perfect, he thought with a smile. Every great wizard had a scepter, and now he had one too. He looked down at his reflection in the water, held the scepter at arms length, and placed a fisted hand heroically on his other hip. Looking at himself in the glassy surface of the puddle, he hoped that the wind might suddenly pick up and cause his tattered clothes to flicker like flames behind him. When the wind didn't come, he raised the scepter over his head with both hands and waited for the sky to part and for lightning to bolt down from the clouds.

But nothing happened.

No matter, thought Aidan, with a shrug. Even if he didn't have any magical powers, with the scepter he could at least *look* like a wizard. Now all he needed was long white hair and a beard to match. Luckily this was easy enough to achieve; all he had to do was to be patient and grow old.

He began walking, his new stone scepter clicking out a steady rhythm against the ground underfoot. As he crested the last hill before Garnock, he enjoyed a great view of the village. Most of the dwellings were still standing, although many were leaning to one side, or were buttressed by anything that was handy. Everything that could be saved seemed to be out drying in the afternoon sun, and crews were working hard to get paths and roadways passable once more.

It was good to see, thought Aidan. And even though he wasn't helping rebuild the village, he was reclaiming a few of the useful items that had been lost. The horseshoe he'd found might fit a workhorse hauling timbers, and the cup could be used to bring water to a thirsty road worker.

And the scepter?

For a moment Aidan held it out like an extension of his right arm, passing it slowly from left to right, as if he were casting a spell over the entire village, repairing in an instant all the damage done by the flood. Nothing happened, of course, but Aidan pictured it all in his mind: homes looking as new as the day they were built and roads straight and flat, ready to lead farmers to market.

Aidan sighed wistfully. But when he ran out of breath, the sound of his sigh lingered . . . growing louder. Down in the village, people stopped what they were doing, dropped what they had in their hands, and scattered like spiders caught in the glow of a candle.

The sound of rushing air grew louder still and Aidan turned to see where it was coming from. He looked up and was momentarily blinded by the sun. But then the sun winked out, eclipsed by the bulking outline of a winged dragon.

Aidan's first thought was to run, but his knees had gone weak at the sight of the dragon and were not responding to his wishes. The sound of rushing wind grew to a thundering roar, and an instant later, Aidan was knocked to the ground by a blast of air as the dragon flew over him within an arm's length of his head.

Using the scepter to get back to his feet, Aidan watched the red-hued beast slowly circle over the now empty village. It wheeled around and came diving towards him, its huge teeth-ringed maw open wide and a fire alight in its eyes.

Aidan desperately looked for a rock or a hole where he might find cover, but the hill was flat and grassy and there was nothing but open space around him. His breath getting short, he prepared for the end, planting his scepter in the ground and striking his most heroic pose. If he was going to die, at least he would do it with dignity.

But, instead of burning him to a cinder, the dragon landed gently on its hind legs. For a moment it stared at him, perhaps bewildered that the boy wasn't running in terror.

"Stay away from me!" Aidan said, pausing a moment to clear his throat. "Or else!"

"Or else what?" the dragon asked.

Even though Aidan had heard that some dragons, especially red ones, could talk, he was still surprised at how well this one spoke, and at the deep throatiness of its voice.

"Or – or s-someone will g-get hurt!" he stammered at last.

That made the dragon laugh. It took several steps forward, halving the distance between them. "Yes-s-s," it hissed. "But that's the point, isn't it?"

Aidan did not move. Even when the dragon came closer, he stood his ground. A great wizard didn't run from a dragon, and neither would he. He took the scepter in both hands and held it before him like a club. It wasn't much of a weapon against a dragon, but it was all he had.

"Careful with that, boy," said the dragon. "You might poke somebody's eye out."

Yes, thought Aidan. *Poke it in the eye, or another vulnerable spot on its body – the belly perhaps.*

The dragon must have thought Aidan a curiosity because it moved even closer, inspecting him as if he were a piece of jewelry under glass. Aidan realized that the dragon did not fear him in the least, and if he was going to strike out at it, he'd have to do it quickly, to make use of the element of surprise.

As the dragon opened its mouth to speak, Aidan turned the sharp end of the scepter towards it and lunged awkwardly at the belly of the beast. At first the dragon seemed surprised by Aidan's move, but it quickly recovered and stepped aside. Aidan's blow missed the mark, and the scepter glanced harmlessly off the beast's hind leg.

The dragon smiled mockingly. "That the best you can do?"

Aidan stood his ground, wondering if he should strike again or run for it. He decided that he wouldn't get far if he ran, so he brought the scepter forward and prepared for another attack.

But then a strange thing happened.

The spot where the scepter had touched the dragon's body began changing color, turning from red to gray. And the spot grew as well, the gray color expanding out to cover more and more of the leg.

The dragon's eyes and mouth opened in surprise. It let out a sharp scream and reached for its leg, which by now had changed into solid rock! As its claws took hold of the stone leg, they too turned to stone, helping to speed up the transformation, until its entire body was hard and gray and still. The screams continued until the beast's mouth and throat were stone as well, and then they slowly died out.

The only sound was that of the wind blowing over the top of the hill. It picked up for a moment, blowing the stone dragon over onto its side. The ground shuddered and several bits of stone broke away from the dragon's body.

After that, all was still and silent.

Aidan took a deep, shaky breath, the first in some time.

In the distance the villagers were beginning to appear

– just a few at first, then more and more. They were running towards him and they were cheering.

He swallowed. Somehow he had saved the village. With his scepter. His magic scepter.

"He slew the dragon!" someone shouted.

"He's saved the village from total ruin!"

The crowd flowed up the hill, circling him and patting him on the back, while children fearlessly climbed atop the stone dragon as if it were a favorite tree.

"Three cheers for Aidan!"

"Hurrah! Hurr –"

"He's no hero!" The voice was loud and strong, immediately silencing the crowd. "He's just a boy! A little scavenger boy who was in the right place at the right time."

The voice was that of Cormick Skerry, the wizard of Garnock. With his long white hair and sparkling long robes, he was a striking figure of a man. As a result, he was much respected by the villagers, and his words carried great weight.

"Indeed, he did slay the dragon," said Dempster, the village baker. He and Aidan's father had been good friends and sometimes he gave the boy free bread when he was hungry. "And we all saw him do it, too."

Cormick shook his head. "You saw the dragon fall, but it wasn't because of the boy."

"What was it then?" asked Dempster.

Cormick took a small leather pouch from within the folds of his robe and held it up for all to see. "For weeks I've been sprinkling this into the dragon's wellspring. As you can see, it eventually worked its magic."

The villagers looked over at the dragon, then at Aidan. Finally, their gaze returned to Cormick.

"The boy just happened to be there when the potion took effect," said the wizard. "I am the one who saved the village, not the boy."

The crowd was silent, considering Cormick's words.

No, Aidan thought angrily, shaking his head. *It can't be.* The dragon began turning to stone at the exact spot where the scepter had hit it. While it was true that Cormick was a master at mixing herbs and powders, he had been nowhere near the dragon these past few days. Obviously, he was lying.

It was also clear that the villagers were having trouble believing Cormick, but they respected him too much to say so out loud.

"I did it," Aidan protested. "I *was* the one!"

But by then few were listening. The moment of triumph had been lost, stolen out from under him by Cormick Skerry. The crowd slowly began to break up and return to the village. A few men came by to pat Aidan on the back, saying, "You did good, son," but their quiet words only made him angry.

"I *was* the one," he muttered to himself as the crowd drifted away. "It *was* me!"

He walked over to the stone dragon and leaned against it. As he looked over the great stone mass, a faint smile began to break over his face. Although Cormick had stolen the credit for slaying the dragon, he'd at least had a taste of what it would be like to be a real wizard. He liked the feeling. Now he was more determined than ever that someday he would become a real wizard. Someday soon.

Aidan laid the scepter down on the soft straw that would be his bed for the night. It was a comfortable enough stable, and no one seemed to mind that he'd been sleeping in it for months. Of course, since he had been the one to slay the dragon, he *should* have been sleeping in the inn tonight, on a down-filled bed with a real pillow. But, since Cormick Skerry had claimed he had been the one to rid the village of the dragon, Aidan had to settle for a free loaf of bread and a pitcher of sweet water. It was no night's sleep in the inn, but as his father had said many times before he died, it was better than a kick in the pants with a frozen boot.

Aidan gathered several handfuls of straw and bunched them behind his head. Then he lay back, closed his eyes, and immediately fell asleep.

He was awakened by a slight jostling movement to his arm. He opened his eyes and, through the hazy veil of sleep, saw a figure pulling on the scepter that was tucked under his arm. Even in the darkness, and half-asleep, he recognized the figure as Cormick Skerry.

Quickly he grabbed the scepter with both hands and used it like a staff, pushing the heavy end forward and striking Cormick a hard blow to the head. Cormick yelped once and fell to the ground, but managed to grab a handful of Aidan's coat. Aidan struggled to get free, striking Cormick's hand with the scepter, and finally breaking away when one of his pockets was torn from the old coat.

Aidan could hear Cormick's curses, but did not dare stop to look behind him. He dashed out of the stable into the village square and vanished among the crowd, who was still out celebrating the death of the dragon. Although he'd gotten away and it seemed safe enough, he kept on running through the night . . .

Up on the hill overlooking Garnock, the stone dragon grew warm beneath the light of the morning sun. Although there was no one there to see the movement, the stone began to tremble slightly, as if it were a giant egg getting ready to hatch.

As the sun rose higher and the day grew hotter, a small line formed along one side of the stone dragon's head. Slowly the crack got bigger and wider, until pieces of rock and rubble began to fall from the dragon's head like tears of stone.

By midmorning the crack had grown bigger and, through a wider section of the break, a large black and yellow eye looked out, angry and eager for revenge.

Aidan had walked through the night and into the next day, heading eastward away from Garnock. Although he couldn't see anyone following him, he could feel a presence some distance behind. The scepter, too, seemed to feel something alien, for it hummed in his hand as if coursing with nervous energy.

Once again he turned and looked back in the direction of Garnock. He could see no one, but the feeling was getting stronger, as if someone was getting closer. And that someone could only be Cormick Skerry. Obviously the scepter did possess some real magic, and the wizard craved it for himself.

Aidan shook his head sadly. Cormick Skerry had always been his hero, the one villager he wanted to grow up to be like. Yet here he was, trying to steal something from a little scavenger boy, the orphan son of the shoemaker. A great wizard acting no better than a common thief!

As Aidan trudged wearily on he began to smell the sea. Had he been walking for that long? He stopped and looked east, seeing that the horizon was now the deep blue color of the sea. He'd reach the coast soon. Then what was he to do?

Behind him, he felt Cormick getting closer, his presence now like hot breath on the back of his neck. He turned quickly and for the first time saw the figure of a man walking towards him. With a menacing scowl on his face and fiery anger in his eyes, the long flowing hair and trailing robes were undeniably those of Cormick Skerry. Aidan wanted to run, but there was nowhere for him to go, except into the sea . . .

After lunch Dempster and some of the other villagers walked up the hill to take another look at the stone dragon. To their amazement they found the stone broken and scattered over a wide area. Several of the larger rocks looked like pieces of the dragon – a claw here, half a snout there – but for the most part, the rock had crumbled as if the dragon had turned to dust during the night.

But, as Dempster looked more closely, something about the remains didn't sit right with him. If he was to gather up all the rocks and dust and pile them together, it wouldn't be nearly enough to make up a whole dragon.

Which left him with a question. Where did the rest of the dragon go?

Aidan turned away from the wizard and felt the cool sting of sea mist on his face. He stood on the cliff edge and looked desperately down at the roiling sea below. It was a long way down – too far to jump – and anyway, he couldn't swim. If he fled to the north or south along the cliff, Cormick would catch him. No, he'd have to turn back and confront him, face-to-face.

"Give me the scepter, boy!"

The voice was so close Aidan could feel the words in the pit of his stomach. Slowly he turned to face the wizard.

"I said, give me the scepter!"

Aidan held it firmly in his hand. "No!"

"Its power is wasted on you."

"I found it," Aidan said defiantly. "It's mine."

"It needs a wizard to channel its power. I can —"

"You're no wizard!" Aidan retorted defiantly.

Cormick was silent for a moment, as if considering Aidan's words. At last he sighed and said. "I'm getting tired of this, boy!" He took a step closer. "Give it to me now!"

"Never!"

"Very well, then I'll *make* you give it to me."

Aidan felt a shiver of fear run down his spine. He'd never heard Cormick speak so threateningly before, nor seen this madness in his eyes. It frightened him, and it also sickened him. Cormick Skerry, the great "wizard," threatening a young boy who had done nothing in his life but admire the wizard's greatness.

Cormick moved closer, his gnarled fingers reaching out like talons towards him. There was a smile on his face, a wicked smile that suggested he would enjoy tearing the boy apart limb from limb to gain the scepter.

As he looked at the anger and madness in the old man's eyes, Aidan realized he no longer wanted to become a wizard. Not if it meant having to lie and steal and threaten those around him. He was the son of a simple shoemaker. So what! His father had been a hard-working man who'd never done a dishonest thing in his life. He couldn't say the same for Cormick. His robes were beautiful, he spoke like a nobleman, and he was wealthy and powerful.

But to threaten a boy — and for what? For a stone scepter. A length of stone.

It had already done its job, Aidan decided. It had saved

Garnock from the dragon. Aidan would have liked to keep it, but he didn't really need it any more.

So rather than have the scepter snatched from him by Cormick, he reached back and flung it far over the cliff into the sea.

The scepter sailed end over end through the air before straightening out and plunging like a needle through the surface of the water. There was a tiny splash and the scepter was gone. Lost forever.

"Stupid, stupid boy!" screamed Cormick, falling to his knees.

Not stupid, thought Aidan. He knew he'd done the right thing.

Until he heard behind him the distinctive whisper of dragon's wings, and looked up to see the outline of the red dragon streaking across the plain towards them.

Wh∂t if . . . you could breathe life into paper?

PAPER
Marcel G. Gagné

Fascinated, Daniel followed his grandmother's old fingers while they deftly wove magic in their mathematical dance. Wrinkled folds of skin, draped almost casually over her old bones, moved in ways that mocked his young, but clumsy, fingers. Every motion was elegant choreography, each fold an artful rendition of an exact science. Two days of insistence had finally convinced her to share her secrets. This was the initiation. Her price was his rapt attention.

Displays of her handiwork were everywhere. A veritable menagerie of birds, fish, flowers, and even entire scenes spread throughout the house. One shelf displayed a barnyard diorama complete with pigs, horses, chickens, and a farmer watching over them all. On another shelf, she had gathered a full orchestra. Before the assembled musicians, the black-clad conductor stood on a podium, his baton held high. Other objects were strictly decorative: strange boxes and shapes of various colors. She, herself, wore a pair of earrings from which dangled two identical deep-purple birds.

This week of forced confinement with his grandmother was turning out to be interesting after all. Daniel could almost forgive his parents for abandoning him while they took a holiday on their own.

The paper opened briefly and collapsed again under her fingers as she worked the crease to a point that had not existed before. "That's called a petal fold," she said. "This point could just as easily be one of the bird's wings as its head and tail. In a more difficult design, it could become the head and tail of a dinosaur."

A smile of wonder crossed Daniel's lips. "Yeah!" he breathed. The lumbering crash of a great beast sounded in his imagination, the mental camera panning up and down to catch the terrible gaze of the prehistoric monster. Heart-pounding background music accompanied its ear-splitting roar.

"Will you do the dinosaur, Grandma? *Please.*"

"That's a little bit harder than what we're working on here. You have to walk before you can run," she said.

His smile turned to a frown. "Aw, c'mon, Lorraine!" he ventured.

Lorraine put the model down and pierced Daniel's eyes with her own. "*What* did you call me?" The old woman held a great deal of power in those eyes. Daniel shrank beneath the steady gaze.

"That's what Dad calls you," he explained.

"Your father is thirty years older than you are. When you get to be forty, then you can call me Lorraine, but right this minute, I am Grandma to you. Understand?"

Daniel nodded wordlessly.

"Now, where were we?" She carefully picked up the paper model.

"We were going to build a dinosaur," Daniel attempted.

She gave a small laugh. "Nice try, but first things first. This particular fold will become the classic Japanese crane."

"But a bird is so boring. A dinosaur at least looks like it could *do* something."

"Birds look like they can fly. That's something, too. Let's finish this and then you can tell me if it was boring. Until then, observe."

She finished one side, turned the model over and stopped halfway through what she called a kite fold. She looked at him and smiled. "You try it."

Daniel shook his head, an uncertain smile crossing his lips. "No, I couldn't do it like you do."

She took his hands and directed them to the folded paper. "Yes, you can. Just follow the pictures in the book," she said, tapping the open volume on the table before her. The book was at least three inches thick and contained thousands of step-by-step diagrams of hundreds of paper creations.

Daniel ran his fingers over the paper. The multicolored sheet had a clothlike texture. He smiled and looked up. "It feels neat."

"A friend who taught me, as I am teaching you, sent them to me." She touched the package and a faraway look entered her eyes. "These are special papers. Very special."

"What makes them so special?"

She reached out to touch his chest with her index finger. "They echo whatever is in your heart. That is why your heart must be filled only with good thoughts and beautiful things. *Honi soit qui mal y pense.*" The finger moved to his head. "Remember that."

Daniel looked puzzled. "Remember what?"

"Evil be to him who evil thinks. King Edward III of England said that a long time ago when he felt a lady in his court was being insulted."

With a shrug of his shoulders Daniel let the quiet wisdom slip away. He played with the paper, looking back and forth between it and the pictures in the book, then pushed it away with a sigh.

"You better do it, Grandma. I'll try after you finish this one."

With a disappointed shake of her head, she quickly finished the last folds. The head and tail came down, then a squash fold of the center point held the wings in place. "There." She held the bird up to the boy's eyes and turned it over in her hands.

"Neat!"

Grandma smiled. "See how easy it is? Like magic."

In a blur of sight and sound, the paper bird in her hands was transformed into a brightly colored beating of real wings that quickly took to the air. The bird grew larger and larger as it rose to the cathedral ceiling, whereupon it disappeared as though it had simply passed through an open window.

"Grandma!" the boy shouted. "How did you do that?"

She laid the book down in front of him and passed him a package of square papers of various flat colors. "Everything you need to know is there. Just follow the steps . . ." She waved a hand over the line drawings, ". . . and you'll make your own bird just as I did."

"Will it fly like yours did?"

She gave him a quizzical look. "Fly? Humph. Only in your imagination . . ." She paused, ". . . which is more than enough." She rose to her feet and started to turn away. "I've got things to do now. Practice that one just as I showed you, then we'll work on something more complicated."

"But it flew away! *You* saw it!" he protested.

"I did?" She smiled, her eyes twinkling. "I'll check your work later."

She turned and headed up the stairs, taking her cloth paper sheets with her.

Daniel's first attempts were disastrous. The results of his effort resembled badly folded road maps and not graceful birds, but he was determined to achieve the magic he had witnessed with his own eyes. After two and a half hours of folding and throwing away failed experiments, he managed a respectable imitation of his grandmother's crane.

He tossed the bird into the air and watched it tumble ignominiously back to the floor, never having beat a single wing, not even in Daniel's imagination. He picked up the bright pink creation and repeated the experiment. Again it failed. He looked closely at the model. It *was* pretty shabby. He sighed and began again.

When he finished there were seven birds arrayed on the table. The last, a black bird, was a masterpiece of sharp lines and perfect detail. Proudly holding up the model, he tossed it into the air – and watched it tumble to the ground, just like the others.

He scowled and stared, grimly determined to figure out what the difference was between his creation and his grandmother's. He had followed the instructions step-by-step, and his black beauty was perfect in every detail.

He left the rainbow flock lined up on the table and went to fetch his grandmother. It was time to ask her why his bird wouldn't fly. Besides, he needed her to tell him how well he'd done.

He could see through the double glass doors that she was in her back garden, planting some purple flowers. His hand was on the door when his memory filled in the missing piece of the puzzle. The cloth papers! Quickly, quietly, he stepped back from the door and ran upstairs to Grandma's room.

The tension was almost more than he could bear. The package of cloth paper was not sitting out in full view as he had hoped. He had searched through all but two of her dresser drawers before he located it hidden under a liner that smelled of roses.

His heart was racing by the time he had completed the bird base. "From here," he recited silently, "you can make a bird or a . . ."

Yes! Excitement replaced his guilty panic. He picked up the book and searched the pages for the right diagram. There were several dinosaurs, but they were small and insignificant. He turned one last page. There it was, standing on its hind legs with two little arms up in front. A *real* dinosaur! He couldn't pronounce its name. He would have preferred a Tyrannosaurus Rex, but this looked enough like one. The others reminded him more of lizards than the terrible beasts of his imagination. Real dinosaurs were fierce, frightening creatures that tore through flesh with razor-sharp teeth. The others were just vegetarians.

"Begin with a bird base," the instructions read. He had a bird base. He was ready.

Each fold that followed was increasingly difficult but, with a perseverance born of a real goal, he pushed on, doing and redoing folds as needed. This project was a whole lot more interesting than a stupid bird.

When, at last, he sat the finished figure proudly in front of him, it took only the sound of the table cracking under its rapidly increasing weight for him to understand that he had made a terrible mistake.

By the time the creature stood at what he could only hope was its final height, Daniel was running for the stairs up to the bedrooms. Nearly ten feet tall and full of primal fury, the young dinosaur was everything he had hoped for. And he remembered it was a carnivore.

Maybe it's not hungry, he told himself weakly.

The beast snarled and growled as it sensed his presence. The tail swung about and collapsed what remained of the table, sending the chairs crashing across the room.

From the stairs, Daniel could see his grandmother running back towards the house. The crash of table and chairs had not gone unheard. As he scrambled upwards, the beast behind him, Daniel felt his leg being jerked back. He screamed and looked over his shoulder. The deadly teeth had pierced his jeans. The monster bashed his leg repeatedly against the stairs, shaking its head furiously in an effort to get rid of the fabric caught in its teeth. Daniel screamed again, this time in pain. Then his jeans tore and his leg was free. He scrambled out of reach of the vicious teeth just as his grandmother entered the room.

"What in the world is going on here?" she gasped.

She was answered with a growl.

"My God, Daniel! What have you done?"

At the sound of her voice, the dinosaur turned its leathery head with lightning speed to face her. For a moment Daniel was forgotten.

She moved back slowly, calculating her odds of beating the dinosaur to the back door.

Daniel suddenly realized exactly what he had done. *She's going to be eaten*, he thought. *And it's my fault.*

He tore off his shoe and threw it at the beast's head. The creature stopped suddenly, momentarily confused, then looked up towards the source of the missile.

"No!" Grandma shouted. "Daniel, don't!"

Daniel wasn't listening. He hurled his second shoe. This time the animal swung around fully, its tail catching the old woman and sending her crashing among the debris of her dining-room furniture. She lay motionless, while the monster turned its attention back to the boy. This time Daniel didn't run. He sat at the top of the stairs, looking in horror at his grandmother, motionless on the floor below.

The dinosaur moved slowly. Its prey wasn't running away. Size and strength were obviously on its side, but it seemed suddenly wary. Daniel crouched on the stairs, waiting for the end. Perhaps his grandmother would forgive him when she saw him again in heaven. But then panic washed over him. Heaven? He'd been really bad, hadn't he? Likely, he would wind up in a very different place than she would.

Something stirred from within the debris.

"Daniel."

The boy turned, startled. Confused, the beast also turned towards the sound.

Grandma was fumbling with her earrings, taking off each one in turn. She carefully tore the hooks from the backs of the twin birds and threw both into the air. Upon leaving her hand, the birds breathed life and took on an olive-brown color. By the time they had reached the dinosaur and began screaming and tearing at the animal's eyes and face, they had grown nearly a foot in length.

A great roar shook the house as the deadly carnivore tried to shake off its attackers. Grandma rose painfully to her feet and carefully approached the screaming, thrashing beast. Her hands wove mysteriously over the animal's skin and, seconds later, she was holding a harmless model of the dinosaur. The birds, a pair of mourning doves, alighted on the banister and stayed there, cooing softly. Meanwhile, she quickly and deftly unfolded Daniel's creation.

"You did good work, Daniel, but I told you to work on birds, not dinosaurs. Furthermore, you did not use the paper I gave you and, worst of all, you went snooping in my room."

Daniel began to cry. "I'm sorry, Grandma. I almost got you killed."

"Not to mention yourself." She was surprisingly calm. "You forgot the king's lesson, and you did not follow mine. I warned you that your heart must be filled with good thoughts."

She walked over to where the boy still sat on the steps and bent down to hug him. She didn't seem old or frail anymore.

"I really am sorry," he sobbed.

"Yes, I'm sure you are. The question now is, how will you pay for the damage you have caused and the trouble you've made for me?"

"I'll work," he said through tears. "I'll get a job and . . ." His plans for repayment were lost in a flood of tears.

"Oh, stop this nonsense," Grandma said briskly. She got to her feet, picked her way through the debris of her former dining room and retrieved the origami book from the rubble. When she returned, she flipped quickly through the pages until she found what she was looking for. "I still have some gardening to do out there, and you have a mess to clean up. Once you've got this room back in order, I want you to work on these." She pointed to the diagrams on the page.

Daniel sniffed and wiped his eyes. The words he read forced him to look around the house once more and wonder.

"Table and six chairs," the heading read.

What if . . . a wizard came back as a snowman?

FROSTY
Jason Kapalka

There must have been some magic in that old black hat they found, for when they placed it on his head he began to curse and howl.

But as soon as he noticed all the children staring up at him in amazement, he calmed right down and apologized and told them he'd just been a little cranky after waking up.

None of the kids had ever seen a live snowman before. It was awfully neat, the way he talked, like his mouth was full of soggy cereal, and the way he walked, with loud scrunching sounds. But he made them promise not to tell their parents, because then he'd have to go away and he wouldn't be able to play with them or tell them stories.

The children swore to die with a needle in their eye before they'd tell, and Frosty (for that was what he said his name was) smiled a little and twinkled his bottle cap eyes.

They asked Frosty how he had come to life, and Frosty said it was a long story, but he'd tell them if they would listen.

They all sat down in a circle around Frosty, out there by the edge of the woods, and he started to speak, his tree-branch arms rustling and cracking.

He told them about a man who had lived in town a long time ago, a man who did fun magic things. But the other people in town were mean and didn't like fun things, so they called him a lot of bad names, and then they took the man and burned him up, because they thought he was a witch. The children were a little confused by now, because witches were ugly old ladies who flew through the air on sticks. Only they didn't burn up everything of the man, Frosty said, not quite everything, and here he stopped and took his hat off and looked mad, though he could have been sad. It was hard to tell with his face all made out of snow.

No one really understood, but the boys liked hearing about the man getting burnt up. One of the girls pouted because she wanted a happy ending. Frosty patted her head and told her that maybe there would be a happy ending, after all, but that would be another story.

It was getting late then, so Frosty told them to go home and come back the next day, but not to tell anyone about him, or he wouldn't talk to them any more. The children crossed their hearts again before they left.

The next day Frosty was very happy. He popped off his head and put it back on, and rolled around on the ground until he was just a great big snowball, and showed them other snowman tricks. He told them how great it was being made of snow, because he could stay out all day and all night in the woods, and he never had to eat vegetables or pork chops. All the kids were jealous.

Frosty made them bring him paper and stuff out there in the woods, though they had to bring him crayons because they couldn't find any pencils. They also brought him a calendar, and Frosty frowned when he looked at it and they told him what day it was. The kids asked him what was wrong, but he smiled and said it was nothing, and would they like to hear another story?

He told them about way back long ago, when all kids ever did was play and there were no such things as bedtimes. But then all the Moms and Dads in the world got together at a big meeting and decided that the children were having too much fun and they had better do something about it. So they invented spankings and cough medicine and school, and forever after they made all the children go to bed by eight o'clock. This was a true story, Frosty whispered.

The story scared the children and made them sad. One little blonde girl was even crying. She told Frosty she wished she could be a snowman too, so she wouldn't have to go to bed, and could have fun all the time. For just a second, Frosty looked like he was angry, terribly angry, and his face crunched up around his bottle cap eyes . . . but then he smiled, sort of, and told her that sometimes it wasn't fun being a snowman. He said that sometimes it was like you had gotten snow inside your boots and your gloves and down your neck, except that you could never go inside and get warm again. The little girl snuffled back a tear and hugged Frosty, because she was sorry for him.

Then Frosty became very serious and told them he wouldn't be around for much longer. The kids were sad when they heard this, but Frosty said not to be, because he'd be back again some day if they did him a special favor after he was gone.

He wouldn't tell them what it was, but when they did it, he said, it would always be winter in the town, or the town would go to where it was always winter, the kids couldn't quite figure it out, but Frosty said it would be great fun.

When they'd done that, then Frosty would be able to come back, and he'd send all the mean parents away for good, and he could play with the children again. *I'll be able to play with you forever*, he said, *forever and ever and ever*.

Sure enough, the very next day was the beginning of spring, and it was warm enough that the snow started to thaw. Suddenly scared, all the children rushed out to see Frosty, and they were almost too late, because he was melting too. Just about all of the girls and even some of the boys started bawling then, since Frosty was dripping and getting slushy, and his bottle cap eyes fell off. With all the water rolling off his face he looked like he was crying.

But Frosty told all the children to be quiet and settle down, and to listen to him carefully. He said there were three things they had to do when he was gone.

The first was they had to take care of his old black hat, very good care, so nothing ever happened to it.

The second thing they had to do was called a *rich-ool*. It was a bunch of pages with Frosty's crayon drawings of stars and funny-looking animals, and lots of words that looked even longer and more complicated than the ones in grown-up books. Frosty said that when the calendar told them it was the right day, they had to read the words and do the things the *rich-ool* told them to. It was getting hard to understand what he was saying, because his mouth was all mushy.

And the third thing they had to do was promise to never, ever tell their parents or anyone else about him or show them the *rich-ool*. *Cross your heart and hope to die*, he said, and he looked really awful now, with pieces of him falling off onto the ground all over, so the children managed to stop crying long enough to promise Frosty they'd do it, they'd do whatever he told them.

At last Frosty seemed to quiet down. He said a few more things, but since his mouth was melted almost right off, no one could understand them. It sounded a little like he was laughing. Finally he fell over and broke up into little pieces, and the pieces shrank away, and then all that was left was his old black hat.

The kids stood around and cried for a bit, but it was getting late and dinner would be ready soon.

They passed the *rich-ool* around to see if anyone could understand it, but it turned out that nobody could read very well yet. They just hadn't had the heart to tell Frosty. They would have asked their parents what it meant, but they had crossed their hearts not to show them. Finally they gave the *rich-ool* to a boy who said he'd take it home, staple it together, put a nice title page on it, and take care of it as if it were the most important assignment his teacher had ever given him. It was soon lost and never seen again.

The little blonde girl took Frosty's hat, and she really meant to take good care of it, but when she tried to put it on her dog's head, he growled and grabbed it in his mouth and ran away. They found it again a few days later, but it was all torn up and covered in dog drool and they had to throw it out.

But still, all the children remembered their snowman friend, though they sometimes forgot some of the stuff he'd done, and sometimes remembered other stuff that he actually hadn't done, and though they never told their parents, when they grew up and had children of their own, they told them all the wonderful story of Frosty the snowman, and how he came to life one day.

What if... famous people were cloned over and over again?

LUKAS 19

Jean-Louis Trudel

"Should I accept?"

As the question hung in the air, Lukas already regretted asking. Why be so eager? What if the answer threw cold water on his hopes? What if it meant giving up what he wanted more than anything else on this world or all the others of the Star Republic?

He didn't care, he thought fiercely, he'd find another way . . .

"My dear born-again friend, my chance-found child, why ask me?" sighed the old man in front of him. "My lamented father always said that those who want advice will just go off and do the exact opposite . . . But no, don't clench those magic fingers of yours. If you insist, heed another of my father's sayings! Don't look a gift horse in the mouth to count its teeth, by all means; however, if you're being paid to accept it, better make sure it's not going to bite."

The teenager addressed by the old Padrino let his hand leap along the varicolored touch-responsive surface of the instrument on his knees. Melancholy snatches of music tinkled in response, giving voice to the mixed feelings Lukas struggled with.

"Very well, Padrino. I think I know what you mean. The offer is so good there must be a catch."

Yet the agent who'd called on behalf of the company had been persuasive, dangling a five year binding contract with all the trimmings. The company promised money, fame, and a security the young musician had never known.

It was hardly worth mentioning the only other offer in the same breath: a six month deal with a small downtown restaurant, well-paid but with no guarantees . . .

"Exactly what I said," nodded the old man, shaking his mane of white hair.

Yet the teenager could not still his misgivings. Why turn down the planet's biggest live entertainment company, with contacts all the way to Earth? Suddenly angry, he smashed down his fist on the touchboard. Discordant tones assailed his ears. Music wasn't everything in his life. He'd had other dreams . . .

When he calmed down he sighed.

"Yes, I guess it's not that simple . . . But, Padrino, what the flare is a horse?"

Lukas stopped in front of the spycam's little black eye, slipped his hand into the pocket of his coat and whipped out a small book, pointing it at the machine's gaze.

Nothing happened.

He laughed curtly. He hadn't really expected to surprise the computer, yet he couldn't help hoping that, somewhere in the machine's innards, a neural node had burned out because of the unforeseen gesture. He smiled as he let the spycam look over the scratched black casing, the clear polymer screen, and the controls of the electronic book so that the computer would know it was not a weapon. Yet Lukas dearly wished he could hold, for just a minute, a real laserpistol in his hand and blast his way out into the real world . . .

"Lukas 19!"

Startled, the teen jumped guiltily, pocketing the book, and turned towards the speaker built into the wall beside the spycam. The computer's voice added, "Lukas 19, the principal wants to see you in his office."

The high spirits of the youth vaporized like snow under a sunflare. For sure the principal wasn't calling him in to discuss the upcoming Planetary Games. Lukas was turning fifteen soon. On that day, the Institute would no longer hold any power over him. It would be the last birthday of his childhood and the first of his new life outside . . .

Yet what would happen to him once he was out? Even if he hated the place, the Institute was safe and familiar.

He had spent all the years of his life in the rooms and corridors watched over by the central computer. Hoping, always hoping that he would be chosen for adoption – and scared at the same time he might have to leave one morning the only home he'd ever known. Now, he mourned the missed chances. The rumors swirling around the dorm about the fate in store for the over-fifteen set were downright scary.

"Good to see you, Lukas 19. Please sit down."

The principal was barricaded behind his chevron-shaped desk. In spite of the slim-drugs he took, the man was visibly overweight. Beneath a layer of fat, chin and lower jaw flowed invisibly into a thick bull's neck. The thatch of brown hair made him look younger than he was. With his clients, the principal's eyes often held a fake, genial warmth, but the look he reserved for his charges always seemed fraught with impatience, as if to say, "What! Haven't I gotten rid of you yet?"

"Good evening, Principal, sir."

Lukas sat down, examining the desk in front of him. The terminal built into the desktop was half-hidden beneath a snowdrift of fiberplast printouts. With a single look, Lukas scanned the entire mess and knew what he had to do.

His gaze stumbled momentarily on the poster laserfused into the wall behind the director. The fluorescent blue letters hurt his eyes even as they grabbed his attention.

"Not sure about your genes? Not sure about having children the natural way? COME TO THE ADOPTION CENTER OF SYBARIS! We have children for all tastes."

Makes it sound as if we're cereal mixes! Lukas scowled, unhappy with the reminder. *Except that some of us cereal mixes failed the taste test* . . .

They had all been taught in class how the genes of both parents combined in a child. However, the throw of the genetic dice could spell disaster. The most dangerous genes for a baby's future could be deleted at the molecular level, but such a choice was an expensive one for a couple. The other solution, which the teacher hadn't needed to dwell on, was adoption . . .

"Lukas 19, you're not listening to me!"

He muttered an apology. The principal restarted smoothly.

"You'll be fifteen in a few weeks, Lukas 19. We will no longer be able to keep you with us. There is simply no market for boys your age. Usually, we sign contracts on behalf of the

unpicked, binding them for a decade or two to selected part-
ners of ours in the retail business with a need for low-grade
human resources."

Low-grade human resources! Such words . . . Lukas almost
snarled, but the principal didn't notice.

"Good, good jobs, and yet we have to put up with ingrates
who try to break their contracts. So very, very futile!
However, we do have other plans for you . . ." A saurian grin
twisted the principal's lips. "They tell me you have a
modicum of musical talent, a good ear, and a gift for impro-
vising. You'll never be a star, of course, but being a backup
vocalist is better than waiting on tables."

The man threw him a sharp glance. "I'm sure you agree,
Lukas 19. So I called you in to tell you the good news: we'll
soon be signing you to a long-term contract with a live entertainment company right here in town."

So that was it, thought Lukas dispiritedly.

The whispers in the dormitory hadn't been lies after all.
His fifteenth birthday would not turn out to be his pass to
freedom. Instead of opening the Institute's doors, it would
merely condemn him to another kind of prison, where he
might serve to fatten yet another bank account.

"You could show some gratitude, young man," added the
principal, acting puzzled by the silence of his charge.

Lukas clenched his fists. The anger boiling within him
burst out, carrying with it all his other frustrations. The
eternal ache of knowing he would never have parents if he
wasn't adopted. The resentments nurtured by a childhood
spent inside a cage, his every move watched by electronic
eyes. And the rage born of a bitter knowledge that he was
nothing more than human property, birthed in a machine
like a robot.

He shook with the unleashing of his furies.

He rose slowly and set down his outspread hands on the crowded desktop. As he leaned over the desk, his fingers crumpled sheets with official-looking letterheads, but he no longer cared. He snared the principal's eyes just like he had cornered rats in the old attic.

"Well?" asked the man, authority leaking from his quavering voice like water from a sieve.

For a brief moment, Lukas was unsettled by the sudden realization that he was almost as tall as the principal, huddled in his armchair. The teen spotted the man's right hand, repeatedly stabbing the button that would summon the monitors. He knew then that he still had time to say his piece, and so his voice rose to a near shout as he replied, "No, Principal, sir. Did you hear that? No! I've had it with saying 'Yes, sir!', 'Very well, sir,' or 'You're right, sir!' Now I'm saying no! And I'll give you fair warning; throw me out the door now if you care for your Institute's good name. Send me elsewhere and I'll make trouble, I'll run away, I'll blacken your reputation . . . Oh, I can't wait to get out, you know, one way or the other. I never ever want to face your ugly mug again!"

Two monitors came in. Lukas closed his fists, but he didn't struggle too hard when they dragged him outside the room. The voice of the principal pursued him into the hall.

"Don't worry for our good name, Lukas 19. Tomorrow morning, I'll see the city's best psychfixer to arrange a little social adjustment session for you. I'm giving you fair warning too, young man. After your appointment, you'll have a better attitude than most robots!"

The threat echoed ominously in the teen's head. A psychfixer! In spite of everything, the idea made a shiver run down his spine.

At the other end of the hall, the monitors released him. One, a part-time instructor who had Lukas in his computer class, shook his head. "Come on, Lukas, I thought you were smarter than that. Why did you let him get to you?"

"He wants to contract me out to an entertainment company!"

The instructor shrugged. "Life is tough for everyone."

"Well, you've done it now," said the other. "We've got to put you in the cooler for the night."

Lukas growled to hide the joy bubbling inside him. His plan, conceived in a flash as soon as he'd spotted the security key in the midst of the mess on the principal's desk, was unfolding right on track.

His limbs were still shaking with the fear he'd felt when he'd seized the key right under the principal's nose. The only purpose of his little act had been to leave with the key inside his closed fist . . . except that it hadn't all been an act. The hate was real enough.

They came to a small door he remembered well.

"In you go, Lukas . . . Good night."

The door whirred shut behind him.

"Let's get to work," he whispered.

Originally, the bedroom given to kids needing to cool down had been assigned to an electronician on call. And that was part of the plan. It meant that the small room was devoid of spycams and provided with a computer terminal.

Lukas had forgotten that the bed would be so short, sized for the seven and eight year olds, since solitude and the dark weren't enough to cow the older children. But he remembered the darkness, a cozy and comforting presence.

The teen turned on the old terminal. A faint glow appeared in the depths of the cubic holotank. When his eyes grew used to the light, Lukas inspected the stolen key. The cylindrical metal shaft was tipped with a square-shaped plug, sparkling with minute optical circuitry. No doubt about it, it was the master key or a copy of it.

He bent over his wrist, ringed ever since he was a tot by a frail bracelet of metal and plastic which had mounted a more efficient guard than an entire army, keeping him within the confines of the Institute. He was so used to it he hardly felt anymore the metal's cold embrace. The superposed metallic strips constituted a thermocouple generating a small electric current from the temperature difference between his skin and the air. The current powered a transmitter set to squeal if the wearer tampered with the bracelet or got too far from the Institute.

The bracelet prevented tots from getting lost in the woods on the Institute grounds. Yet Lukas had long dreamed of shattering this one symbol of the institution before all others. Now he could do better than that. He fitted the key's tip into the appropriate slot. The nanochips inside the key and the bracelet exchanged passwords. And the bracelet sprang open.

Lukas instantly snicked it shut again. It wasn't time yet.

He then sat in front of the terminal. He didn't try to go through the student network, giving instead the access code one teacher had made the mistake of using in his presence. The code was accepted by the sentinel software and Lukas smiled. In spite of his musical recreations, he really craved a career in computing if he managed to escape.

Bypassing the system security was no great feat, but he took it as a portent of greater things. Connecting to the outside communications port, he asked it to access the library system of the nearest city, Sybaris. An answer flashed through the cube.

"REQUEST APPROVED. NO IN-LINE AVAILABLE AT THIS TIME. PLEASE WAIT."

Lukas waited.

All the in-lines were busy. He would have to wait until one was free before getting the answer he wanted. Alone in the dark, he let his mind wander along the chain of causes and consequences which had brought him into being . . .

For childless couples, adoption was a cheaper solution than genetic re-engineering. However, on a planet like Nea Hellas, tamed and colonized by humanity over eight centuries, the accidents and social tragedies which resulted in orphaned and unwanted children were scarcer than sunless days in Sybaris. Cloning, long forbidden but now gaining acceptance, was one solution. Starting with a person's genetic code, the biotechnicians could bring into being as many twins as needed. The embryos grew inside incubators and the babies could then be adopted – though some, like himself, never were.

But the parents . . . Lukas often thought about the parents he'd never had . . .

Faced with adopting a stranger's clone, most potential parents opted for the clones of celebrities, for the inherent promise of talent and guaranteed success. If money was no object, why not buy both a child and a future for the child? Pick her to be a great scientist, pick him to be a dancer. Or an athlete, a singer, an explorer . . .

Unbeknownst to his teachers and keepers, Lukas had learned much. He had hoarded allusions, gathered scraps of forbidden texts from the Sybaris library, and applied pure logic. Little by little he had become certain that he knew too much. If the principal had so much as suspected, his heart would have gone into overdrive. And the man would have fainted outright if he had ever found out that Lukas had uncovered the identity of his "originator," the man who shared his genetic code with Lukas and eighteen Institute "brothers," all adopted years ago.

For he suspected that he was the nineteenth – and last – clone of Lukas Sarakina, a famous musician dead for over a decade. Demand for Sarakina clones was still high when the nineteenth had been conceived inside the Institute's labs, but by the time Lukas had come of age, it had declined to zero and nobody had adopted him.

And the principal had dared to say to his face that stardom was beyond him!

In any event, the principal's words had strengthened his suspicions. The Sybaris Library would provide him with the final proof.

"IN-LINE NOW AVAILABLE."

"SHOW ME THE FIRST KNOWN HOLO OF LUKAS SARAKINA."

A pause ensued, each second an eternity in the bud.

"LUKAS SARAKINA WHEN HE WAS SEVENTEEN."

In front of the teen's eyes appeared the furrowed features of a young man, grim and unsmiling, the forehead half hidden by thick black curls, the mouth clamped shut under a shadowy moustache.

The holograph snapshot also included a fuzzy backdrop Lukas didn't bother to examine. The teen was avidly detailing his future self, captivated by a time-warped mirror telling him that so he had been and so he would be . . .

"Lukas Sarakina," he whispered just loud enough to savor the sound of those syllables.

He'd started to suspect the truth when his teachers had subjected him to endless music lessons when he was more interested in programming. The identical given names had been another clue. Discovering that the popularity of the

original Lukas Sarakina had peaked the year of his birth —
now, that had almost clinched it. The Institute had surely
tried to capitalize on Sarakina's popularity . . .

And, finally, the principal's plans for him had all but confirmed his deductions.

**"YOUR FREE TIME ALLOTMENT HAS EXPIRED. IN-LINE
CLOSING. THANKS FOR USING THE SERVICE OF THE
SYBARIS CENTRAL LIBRARY."**

Losing no time, Lukas slipped into the subprogram in
charge of the entire surveillance network. With every passing second, his trespass came closer to being noticed. There
was no percentage in being fancy, so he merely inserted a
priority request for a global check of the surveillance network, specified for a given time interval the next morning. To
check all the systems, the spycams and infrared detectors
would be deactivated five minutes before dawn.

That was all Lukas wanted. The principal's key would
unlock his bracelet and all the building's doors, including the
one leading to the garage.

Hadn't the principal said he would be seeing the psychfixer in town about an appointment? And if the principal
took his personal skimmer, Lukas was coming along for the
trip, secreted inside the trunk . . .

"A stellar for your thoughts!"

Lukas came back to the present. "I was thinking of the
day I escaped. Already a quarter-year and it still feels like
yesterday."

The old man smiled. "Oh, when I saw you, I thought time
had started flowing backwards and it really *was* yesterday.
There I am sitting on my balcony when I see my old friend
Lukas Sarakina stroll by, in the flesh, as if he hadn't been dead
for over a decade. And Lukas as I'd known him in the flush of

youth, lean and mean and with the eyes of a starving wolf. My heart almost shorted out."

Lukas nodded and didn't ask what a wolf was.

When he had crawled out of the stopped vehicle's trunk, he'd set off at a dead run, putting as much distance as he could between the principal and him. He'd avoided the new downtown, a single circular building like a truncated mountain, financed by the fabulous riches of the Merchanters' League.

Rather, he'd fled into the narrow, tree-lined streets of the old downtown, now run-down and home to humbler dwellings. The ancient facades dated back to the glory days of the Terran Empire, and most boasted remnants of their past splendor, the gleaming chrome inlays besieged by corroded steel and crumbling stone . . . Lukas had wandered through the curving streets till he was well and truly lost.

And then a white-haired man had called out to him, from a balcony with a metal balustrade carved like the wild fronds of a jungle.

The young clone had reached the end of his endurance. For lack of a better idea, he'd accepted the invitation of the man who'd introduced himself as Pedro Gallardo, retired spacer. Over a few cookies and a bottle of wine they had exchanged secrets. Lightheaded after a single glass of the tart *retsina*, Lukas admitted to his origins, once his host had confessed to his. The Bueno-born spacer had come to Nea Hellas a long time ago, befriending the young Lukas Sarakina when the musician was just starting to make a name for himself. Stunned by the coincidence, Lukas hadn't turned down Gallardo's invitation to stay in the spare bedroom for the night.

("Why are you taking me in?" "At my age, being alone gets to you faster than all the pains of the body." Still, the first night, Lukas had reprogrammed the bedroom lock from inside . . .)

The memories made Lukas smile, and his hands whipped across the organ's touchboard. Flashes of light – azure, purple, and fuchsia pink – washed over the bare walls and receded to the sound of shivery bells.

"Padrino, I . . . It's a wonderful offer, but doesn't it sound a lot like the principal's plan for me? Do you think they've managed to track me down?"

The spacer shrugged. "Don't worry . . . I didn't tell you because I wanted to surprise you, but I applied to adopt you three days ago. All I need is your consent. It would make me your legal guardian, and make you a full-fledged citizen of the Star Republic. The Institute couldn't touch you any more. And you could take the company at its word."

"Why didn't you ask *me*?"

"Aren't you happy?"

The anxious note in his voice forestalled the teen's angry protest. Lukas had always dreamed of being a real child – not just a clone up for sale – with parents who would take him on picnics in the olive groves, a mother to hug him, a father to play with in the park . . .

Too late now. He liked his old Padrino, but it would never be the same.

So he lied, if only to repay past kindness. "You'll never know, Padrino! It's . . ."

He smiled, seemingly speechless with joy, and then tore his gaze away from the happiness shining in the old man's eyes. He focused on the contract terms outlined by the company. Though he was inexperienced, the sums involved smelled bad. It was just too much for a beginner called Lukas . . . and too little for the new Lukas Sarakina.

"Padrino, I've decided. I'll take up that small place down-town on its offer."

Lukas had soon discovered his benefactor was hardly rich. Gallardo had nevertheless managed to present his new flat-mate with a chromophonic organ. And the latest model at that. Lukas hadn't bothered explaining music was just a hobby for him. To repay the gift, he'd decided to put his talents to the test. The veteran spacer had called in some favors and gotten Lukas his first gig in one of the city's many tunebars.

At first he'd been a disaster, about as enthralling on stage as an unplugged computer, but he'd improved quickly. He loved the free and easy experimenting, going from table to table if he was tired of the stage. Flashplaying, they called it. The mingling of light and music never grew stale. Later, he'd tried a traditional "bouzouki" lent by a club owner, and the nights he used both the new and the old instruments, he got standing ovations . . .

"Going there always gives me migraines," grumbled the old man. "Too many people and too much noise. But if you're sure, go ahead."

"I want to be free to change my mind later," explained Lukas. And free to go into computing as soon as he got the chance . . .

"Of course, that's why the company was offering you a megastellar contract," remarked Gallardo. "Buying a man's freedom isn't cheap."

Lukas sighed. He was giving up money and the long-term security of the big contract. And for what? In six months, he would be chasing after another gig. Why go to so much trouble when he really wanted something else?

"I don't know . . . Sarakina would have done the same, I guess."

But his "originator" had loved the whole scene . . . It was different for Lukas. Music had always come easily to him, perhaps too easily, for he had preferred tackling the challenges of higher mathematics and symbolic programming. Reward was all the sweeter for the work being harder. If his music-making was a success, he hoped to finance the studies in metaprogramming he yearned for.

"Sarakina . . ." Lukas frowned. "Padrino, you knew him. Was he happy?"

"Now, that's an interesting question. The man isn't born who actually *hates* success. Yet Sarakina often wondered if he might not have been happier doing something else . . . I told him my much-lamented father used to say we're born with a capacity for happiness that cannot be exceeded, the way you can't put an entire bottle of wine into a single glass."

Lukas grimaced. "Your father was wrong! Genes aren't everything. I've always laughed at the buyers who expect the clones of geniuses or brilliant artists to turn out like their 'originators.' They may get luckier with athletes, but scientists and artists will never lead the exact same life as the original. You can't replay a life, with all the incidents and influences which shaped a vocation . . . Come on, Padrino, what do I have in common with Sarakina?"

"More than you think. When I look at you, I have trouble believing you're not Lukas Sarakina, reincarnated by the grace of the Faraway Powers."

Lukas frowned sulkily. He didn't care for the idea of being a mere rerun of Sarakina. He protested. "I'm Lukas 19, the clone for sale! What the flare do I have in common with Sarakina, fortune's favorite?"

"Don't you know what my friend's childhood was like? When he was fifteen, on the verge of being sent to an orbital factory, he ran away from a children's shelter."

"A shelter? How did he end up in a shelter?"

"His parents died in a spaceship accident. Since they were his only relatives within forty light-years, he became a ward of the planetary services."

"The poor guy," whispered Lukas sorrowfully. The only thing worse than not having parents was to have parents and lose them. Then it clicked and he reacted. "But none of the bios mention it!"

"He never spoke of it, true. But that's when he first dreamed of becoming a great metamathematician, spinning theories for a living. However, to put food on the table, he was forced to make the rounds of the downtown bars and dives with his old guitar. What followed, to quote my father, was as unsurprising as the splashing when you heave a stone into a pond."

Lukas wordlessly gnawed a knuckle. His certainty that personal history did not repeat itself was shaken.

The company's offer was now doubly suspect. If the Institute's principal was behind it, was it because the fat man hoped the same sequence of events would lead Lukas to Sarakina's triumphs? The Institute had files on each DNA donor. Had they seen in Lukas 19 an opportunity not to be missed? A star like Sarakina generated revenues which dwarfed by far the combined profits from a dozen adoptions. Did the Institute refuse to let him be adopted in order to push him towards a more bankable career?

Was that why the principal had smiled when speaking of his "plans"?

But there was still one question, one doubt which tore at him. "Padrino, did they let me escape?"

Had it all been part of a plan? Had they known what he was going to do as if he were nothing but a preprogrammed robot?

"You mean the Institute? If they let you escape, they made the biggest mistake of their lives. You're with me now and there's nothing they can do about it."

"I don't want to end up in their power again."

The teen walked to the balcony's door, half afraid he'd recognize a dreaded yet familiar face in the street. But the pavement of fused stone was a gleaming emptiness under the sun's growing flares. The orb of molten gold appeared to sport a pair of fuzzy ears, brighter than even the sun's blinding surface. On Nea Hellas, radiation levels would be up for a few days, and nobody would venture outside as long as the flares outshone the sun.

As Lukas watched, the only living thing in the street was a black cat heading for a nearby alleyway and cannily sticking to the narrow strip of shadows along the base of the walls.

He was being stupid. Lukas sprang back, cutting through the air-curtain, and found himself in the living room's cool air once more.

"Padrino, do you think Lukas Sarakina would have been happier as a mathematician?"

"Who knows? He'd truly wanted to be one. I could feel the sadness within him. All his life, he never missed a chance to work with numbers, even if it meant managing his own affairs when he could have hired financial experts by the dozen. Don't you see, young one? He carried a dead man within himself – the mathematician he could have been – even after he failed the entry test of the Mathematics Academy."

"But didn't he study?" asked Lukas incredulously. Sad? Padrino was joking. Sarakina had surely been devastated.

"What could he expect? Coming from a shelter where second-rate teachers dispensed third-rate training . . . I warned him, but he didn't listen to me. He was so disappointed he never tried again."

Lukas perceived in the spacer's words a truth equally applicable to him. His own hopes for a career in programming were rooted in the same uncertain soil of inadequate courses.

Was he condemned to suffer the same disappointments? Lukas refused to believe it. Yet if it happened, he would surely recognize the truth now, not deny it.

What cruel irony in this unasked gift for music! A talent verging on the exceptional, since it had bloomed in spite of the lackluster training provided by first a children's shelter and then a clone factory . . . almost wasted on Sarakina, who had taken little joy in it.

Then Lukas gazed upon Pedro Gallardo's careworn face and thought of all those without a special gift, without a driving passion. Could their lives be so arid they wanted to live again through another's career? Perhaps Lukas could now understand why Padrino had been so kind . . .

"Padrino, would it please you if I chose a career in music?" *Again* . . . Lukas added silently.

"Choose what you like, my streetborn son."

The teen heard the lie in the trembling voice. The old man added, "Still, I have a gift for you. Open it before you make up your mind. It's yours, whatever you decide."

The old spacer left to get something in his bedroom, returning with a package.

Lukas unwrapped it slowly. It was a "bouzouki," its wooden curves glistening. The teen's eyes surreptitiously scanned the small flat and noted the absence of an ancient hand-painting once fixed to the wall over the computer terminal. So that was how Padrino had found the money!

A clone dreamed for himself, first and only, but those childhood dreams could be postponed. Lukas knew that he would not give up on them as easily as Sarakina had. However, to be human was to respect the dreams of others . . .

"Padrino," he said proudly, "one day, the whole planet will listen to me play this for you."

WhAt if . . . a record of Earth's last days drifted
out into the galaxy?

THE BOOK OF DAYS

Lesley Choyce

The People did not have very many laws about fishing.
Usually anything at all that was found in space could be kept.
In fact, there wasn't a great deal out there to find. Once you
left the neighborhood of the outer planets, space was largely
empty. Maybe you might find one molecule of oxygen or, if
you were lucky, a speck of silicon dust. But even that was
something to a true fisherman.

The People were great collectors of anything found in
space. Every home had a special room for fishing trophies.
But almost everyone on the planet admitted that their sun
system was just about fished out. Some got lucky and discovered a very small asteroid that they could take home. Others
continued to collect silicon dust or radioactive particles just
for sport.

But there was one law that everyone had to abide by: if
you caught anything in space that belonged to anyone else,
you were obligated to give it back. The People were great

givers and takers. Loaning and borrowing was the most sacred thing in their world. They had all manner of ancient laws about lending and borrowing. But none were ever enforced because it was unnecessary. You gave away whatever you possessed and it was always returned in one way or another. It happened automatically. Since hardly anything was ever found in space that belonged to anyone, however, fishermen were free to keep their catch. But then came the problem with Reese.

Reese had found plenty of nothing in space for years and years. He was one of the worst fishermen ever to live among the People. And it was probably Reese's own fault. He fished remote areas that were far from the sun. He was bored by cosmic dust and molecular clusters of trace elements. Reese liked deep space and didn't mind vast sectors of nothing. He liked fishing for fishing's sake.

And then, one day, Reese was out cruising, looking for anything that presented itself, happy to be companion to all the emptiness, when he found something.

The something was a probe. A small cylinder, maybe a yard across with spikes sticking out. Reese could not believe his luck. He circled the probe, then came up behind it and slowed down to follow it at its own speed. The speed of the probe was almost zero. It was drifting. Reese knew that in deep space speed was rather relative, and he calculated that it had long since run out of whatever fueled it. Now it just kept going because nothing had got in its way to stop it. And here it was. In his own backyard.

So Reese reeled it in without a fight.

During the last years of life on Earth, folks became very interested in leaving some chronicle of who they were. For posterity, you might say. They wanted to leave evidence: a record of their individual identities, what their jobs were, what they had learned, and their thoughts about life in their neighborhood and on Earth. Some rented lockers in old mines that tunneled far down into the earth, because they hoped that someday another generation would excavate and find evidence of their existence. Writers sent books down into the earth, filling up old coal mines; film directors paid vast sums of money to store movies down there. All the old mines were filling up.

This was after everyone had given up the idea of saving themselves and their families. Oh, a few folks tried to chase off into space and find another place to live, but it was very expensive to leave Earth and often it didn't work out. At first, the mines seemed like a possibility for human retreat when the big moment came, but the new weapons took care of that. When the Deep Threat system was approved for development by one side, it was approved on the other. And so there was no place left to stick your head in the sand. Either you went off into space and died up there in a tin can, or you just hung around and made the best of things until the end. Even space seemed an unlikely place to survive; so far, all of the colonists had ended up dead or returned home, preferring to take their chances on the good old surface of the planet after all.

Chris Day lived a quiet life in the suburbs of New York, five hundred miles from Manhattan. He had a good job as a research scientist. His main specialty was trees and why they died. All the trees were dying and there hadn't even been a war yet. He pondered on this for a living. Chris Day had a really nice wife, Camille, and two kids. His son Hickory was nine, and his daughter Willow was eight. They were a sort of new breed of happy-right-up-to-the-end family because that's the sort of folks they were.

Earth was a mess and everything was irreversible . . . or so it seemed. The oceans had risen as predicted. New Manhattan sat on the water and would rise with the new levels. There were no trees left there, of course – no room in the new city, no soil.

All of the professionals in the sciences these days studied the end of things. The Save the Whales, Save the Seals, Save the Frogs, Save the Flowers, Save the Trees movements had all died off. People were becoming more realistic. There was a lot to be learned about the way things stopped existing.

Of course, the men and women who came up with new weapons were still around, dreaming up Deep Threat, Space Chasers, and a whole bunch of other things they had up their sleeves. Everyone was in one way or another working on, or studying, the end of things and watching the news at night to see if anybody had lit the first firecracker that would call for the curtain.

When the entrepreneurs came up with the notion of sending family probes into space, the public loved the idea. They weren't really probes, because they weren't going to find anything. Except maybe an audience. Or so everyone hoped . . . But who or what?

Now Chris Day came home with the paper one day and showed the ad he had come across in the *Times* to Camille.

"It looks like a lot of money," Camille said.

"We have a lot of money," said Chris. "Besides, what are we saving it for?" This was a common thing for all of the elders to say. The end of the world was doing great things for the consumer economy. Nobody saved money at all anymore.

What would be the point? Many families (but not the Days) spent well beyond their credit limits, counting on the end of the world to occur before full payment was due. The banks didn't even seem to mind.

But the Days had saved a little and could borrow a lot. They were waiting for something just like this. A chance to send a record of the existence of their family off into deep space. The price was high: all of Chris Day's salary from that day up to the end except for a small subsistence allowance. In return, the Days would be able to send a half-hour video disk, a documentary of the daily life of their family – off into the frontiers of space.

It would be like living on forever. Long after the end. Sort of.

So Chris Day picked a Saturday in May. He got out the home video camera, popped in a fresh platinum disk, and started filming Hickory and Willow on the swing set. (Hickory and Willow had been given those names because hickory and willow were two of the species of trees still alive. At least they were when Hickory and Willow were born.)

Chris Day filmed Camille in a new dress smiling up at the sun. He took five minutes of Willow walking along a balance beam and falling off only twice. He then filmed Hickory riding his bicycle over the lawn, where the grass had all died. The grass, however, had been sprayed with that rubbery green grass preserver, which made any lawn look almost as good as the real thing.

Chris Day started feeling really creative and he climbed up onto the roof of the house and filmed his backyard with his family just sitting down at the patio table playing MONOPOLY. Then he climbed down, set up a tripod, and filmed himself kissing his wife. Behind them the two children were doing handstands on the permanent green grass.

Camille suggested they take a picture of everything they owned, so Chris started filming some footage of his car in the driveway. He was just zooming in on the steering wheel when Camille yelled something, told him to stop. "I changed my mind," she said. "Let's just do us. Forget the car and the vacuum cleaner." So they forgot the car and the vacuum cleaner, and went back to handstands and kisses and whatever else they could think of. Oh, they filmed themselves eating a meal. The tripod was put up and the table was set. It wasn't even dinnertime, but they ate a big meal together. The dialogue was great:

"Pass the salt, please."

"I really loved the way you cooked the asparagus."

"Could I have some more hothouse yams?"

Everyone pretended the food wasn't artificially produced.

The Days went for a walk to the park, but decided against filming. There was a lot of fighting there and too many motorized toys. They went back home and filmed a family discussion that went like this:

Chris Day: "What do you like most about the end of the world, Hickory?"

Hickory: "I like the fact there won't be any more school."

Camille: "What about you, Willow?"

Willow: "I like the fact that we'll all go together."

"Hmm," said Chris and stopped filming for a minute. Camille put her arms around the two kids. Chris put one arm around the whole family and filmed them hugging. Then he put the kids to bed and filmed them falling asleep. They looked so peaceful.

In the morning Chris took the video disk in to the entrepreneur. Space Legacy was in an upscale neighborhood with several preserved "living" trees. Chris Day signed away most of his salary for the rest of his born days and got in receipt a guarantee that his disk would be sent off in a private-sector launch vehicle a week from Thursday, assuming the world lasted that long. It would be dispersed with a dozen other probes and directed towards the Horsehead Nebula.

"But there are no guarantees that anyone will ever see it," the entrepreneur said. He knew that it was just a courtesy on his part. No one who walked into the store ever changed their mind. "But you can watch the launch on your TV at home. We'll pipe it over channel 77."

"Thanks so much," said Chris, and he went home.

Not long after the ginkgo trees stopped growing new shoots, a power failure somewhere in a Far North alert station tripped some signal or other, and there was a lot of confusion high up with the people who were still studying the best way to end the world. So things didn't go quite as planned. But the effect was good enough.

When Reese the fisherman opened up the probe and saw the platinum disk, he knew that he had discovered something of true significance. He knew he had not been fishing emptiness for nothing.

He took it home and called around to borrow every sort of decoding instrument in the neighborhood until he came up with something that gave him not only sound, but a picture. Reese sat down in a dark room and watched the picture begin to come into focus on the wall. He was alone and it was the biggest moment in his life. "Hi," a smiling man was saying to him. "We're the Day family and this is who we are." The camera work was jerky and a little out of focus.

Reese watched the images on the screen: a little girl skipping rope, walking on a balance beam; a boy hanging upside

down on a swing set; people kissing, hugging, sitting down
to a table, and eating food. It went on and on, but Reese was
entranced, lost in the moment. Finally the kids fall asleep.

The voice came back on: "I don't know if anyone will
ever see this, but we wanted to give it a try. We're the Day
family – Chris, Camille, Hickory, and Willow – and we live
at 4700 Dutch Elm Street in Culloden. That's just off the
Number 7800 Highway North. Well, good luck to you,
whoever you are."

And then darkness.

Reese was so excited he forgot to eat for two days. He
didn't know what to do, so he went back out into deep space
to fish for awhile. And think. He had seen the most incredible thing. In his world, everyone lived alone. It was the way
things had always been. They shared and borrowed, but
none of the People had ever lived with another of the People
like in the pictures on his wall.

After a week of fishing around in the emptiness and watching the video over and over alone in his fishery, he knew
there were two things he must do. First, he had to share his
discovery with the People. Then he had to return the find to
whoever had sent it in the first place.

The People were not fully ready for the Day family. But
the disk was dubbed and redubbed and found its way into
nearly every home on the planet. Everyone watched it
alone and, afterwards, cried or laughed or shouted or fell
down screaming.

A girl walking on a balance beam; a boy riding a bicycle
around in a circle; a man staring into the lens of a camera;
people sitting down to eat together; Willow and Hickory
asleep; and the quavering voice of a man at the end. Above
all, they lived together in a single dwelling!

Reese became a controversial figure for his find. Loved or hated, feared or emulated. More and more of the People went out to the fringes and began deep space fishing. That was not so strange. But then some started going out in pairs.

The President of the People called up Reese, who was still anchored in the zone where he had found the probe. A phone call from the President was an absolute first for Reese.

"You know what you are obliged to do now," the President said. "Not that you haven't done enough already."

"I know," Reese answered, not surprised to receive the reminder even from the President.

"Well, a thing found is a thing found," the President said. "And now a thing has been borrowed and used . . ."

"And I need to return it."

"Right. And thank you," the President said, and the screen went dark.

So Reese gave himself one day to sort out particulars at home, to calculate directions and speed and so on. Many famous people phoned up offering to help, but Reese worked alone. No one had ever before had a destination beyond the fringe. Many had gone deep sea fishing and found nothing but fragments. Reese had found a whole thing.

The idea of time worried him. How long had the probe been out there? What would he find on the other end of his voyage? Would he even live long enough to return the disk? But then he watched the images again. The smiling, the hugging, the fun. It would be worth the effort to go to a place like that. Even if it had changed. Reese took a hot bath and dreamed he was in the backyard with the Day family.

The journey was not as long as expected. Soon he began to receive sound messages, then video transmissions. All, he knew, were from years ago. But the closer he came, the more recent were the messages. One day he was hearing Earth TV and radio broadcasts from thirty years ago, the next, sounds from a decade ago.

And then there was only static.

He circled the planet once and knew he had the right place. But his heart was filled with sadness. Maybe the shroud was always there. Maybe it was a protective covering.

He came in low and began to read the land masses and the oceans, finding that everywhere looked more or less the same. Ash and rubble. But when he landed he discovered there were figures walking about in the rubble. They did not look quite like the Day family. And none smiled. He stopped and asked a man if he knew the Day family and where he could find them.

"Have you come to take us away?" the man asked, his face a mask of injuries.

"No. I just need to return something to the Day family."

The scene would repeat itself many times until he found a mere shadow of a woman, who said that she knew where Culloden used to be.

Reese thanked her profusely and went on. Then, at long last, he found Dutch Elm Street and the property where the Days had filmed the amazing record of their lives.

The house was not there, nor the permanent green grass. Part of the car, though, still sat in the driveway and someone had built something like a small stone fortress alongside it.

"I'm looking for the Day family," Reese said. He tried to make himself sound cheery.

A woman's head poked out of the stone fort. "We're all that's left. What do you want?"

Another head poked out, this time that of a man. Reese could only stare at them. He knew who they were. How could he not help but recognize them, even though they were older?

"Willow? Hickory?" The words sounded strange in his own ears.

The two hunched figures climbed out of the stone fort and looked at him. He held out the platinum disk. Reese saw the surprise, the fear. Then there was hope and, soon, resentment. It hit him hard. At first he did not completely understand. Then it clicked. He had been tricked. The video had just been something false, something made up. It could not have been real at all.

Reese set the disk on the dented, rusting hood of the old automobile and turned to go. He had been made a fool of. "You should not have done this to me," he said in anger. "You should not have done this to the People." He turned to leave, but then grabbed the disk again. He tried to smash it against a rock, but his hand was grabbed by Willow.

"Wait!" she said. "Don't go."

Reese stopped and stood stone-still.

"Will you show it to us?" she asked.

"No," shouted Hickory. "It was not supposed to turn out like this. It was all supposed to end."

Reese looked puzzled.

"Nothing ever does end; it was wrong to think it would so easily. I want to see our family again," Willow said. She was so thin and frail, she seemed to bend in the wind.

"I can show you," Reese said, though he didn't understand what they meant about the end, about what went wrong.

Reese had to stop the video several times because it made Willow and, finally, Hickory cry. Reese could not figure it out. Had they not played a trick on him? Had they not made up ghosts for parents and imagined a house and a backyard, then planted the idea of living together in the mind of the People?

Afterwards, Hickory and Willow got up to leave the ship. Reese took the disk and placed it in Willow's hand. She accepted it and held it to her chest.

"Why did you send that to me?" Reese asked Hickory.

"Because," Hickory answered, "we wanted something to last forever. We wanted something to last beyond the end."

"And now?"

"And now," answered Willow, "we have what we have. What we didn't know was that, for us, the end would go on and on. Like this."

"Maybe you are mistaken," Reese said.

"Please go," Willow said. "Thanks for sharing the Day family with us again."

The disk was still held firmly to Willow's chest.

Reese longed to return to the comfort of the fishery. He rose from Dutch Elm Street and departed from Earth. He set a course for deep space. He did not want to return to his part of the Horsehead Nebula for a long time.

What if . . . water were the most valuable
commodity in the galaxy?

THE WATER TRADERS' DREAM

Robert Priest

All the water traders
 who trade in outer space
 talk of a distant planet –
a magical, mystical place
that has seas and seas full of water,
sweet water beyond all worth.
 They say that planet is green in the sun
and the name of that planet is Earth.

And the people there drink the water,
 they dive and swim in it too.
 It falls from the sky in water storms
 and it comes in the morning as dew.
That sweet, sweet water is everywhere –
 Sweet water! Sweet water of Earth!
 And the traders say that the people there
 have no idea what it's worth.

So the traders have their earth dreams.
 They dream of one silver cup
  brought back across space from the earthlings
 for millions to drink it up.
'Sweet water! Sweet water! Sweet water of Earth!
 The people there trade it for gold!
  They've no idea what water's worth –
 just look how much they've sold!'

They dream the dream of a water storm –
 surely it would drive one mad
  to have a wind-full of water flung in your face,
 to sail in it like Sinbad!
Yes, they say there are whole oceans there
 where waves break on the shore,
  where winds leave water singing
 and the sunlight makes it roar!

They say that those who live there
 just don't know its true worth.
  They say that planet is green in the sun
 and the people there call it the Earth.

ABOUT THE CONTRIBUTORS

Alison Baird's first poem was published when she was twelve years old. Her children's fantasy novel, *The Dragon's Egg*, was nominated for the Ontario Silver Birch Award. She has also published short fiction for adults. Alison Baird has been fascinated by space ever since she watched the live coverage of the Apollo missions as a child. She lives in Oakville, Ontario.

Edo van Belkom is the author of over one hundred and twenty short stories of science fiction, fantasy and horror and of two novels, *Wyrm Wolf* and *Lord Soth*. Edo van Belkom always knew he wanted to be a writer, but turned to writing science fiction and fantasy after reading Ray Bradbury's short story collection *The October Country*. He lives in Brampton, Ontario,

Lesley Choyce has worked as a rehab counselor, freight hauler, corn farmer, journalist, newspaper boy, and well digger. He is a publisher, TV host, editor, and author of forty books including *Good Idea Gone Bad*, winner of the Ann Connor Brimer Award. He also surfs, even in the Nova Scotia winter. He enjoys writing science fiction and fantasy because there are so few limits to the imagination.

Joan Clark lives in Newfoundland. She is the author of seven children's books. *Wild Man of the Woods* (from which "The Mask" is excerpted) was written in a cabin on a small lake in the East Kootenays, to which she returns as often as she can. Joan Clark finds "the line between the natural world and the fantastic hardly exists" and that "sometimes we need fantasy to tell the truth."

Charles de Lint is a full-time writer and musician who makes his home in Ottawa, Ontario with his wife, MaryAnn Harris. Charles de Lint has won numerous awards including the 1988 Aurora Award for Best Work in English for the novel *Jack, the Giant Killer*. His most recent novel is *Someplace to be Flying*. For more information about Charles de Lint, visit his website at www.cyberus.ca/~cdl.

Sarah Ellis is a Vancouver, British Columbia writer who morphs into a librarian by day. She writes a column on Canadian children's books for *Hornbook*. She is also the author of several young adult books including *Pick-Up Sticks* (for which she won the Governor General's Literary Award for Children's Text), *Out of the Blue* and *Back of Beyond* (a short story collection from which "The Tunnel" has been selected). She usually writes about the here and now, but sometimes her interest in fairies leads her into stranger territory.

Marcel Gagné lives, writes, and occasionally edits in the mythical city of Mississauga, Ontario. When it becomes necessary to work in the real world, he takes on the guise of a mild-mannered computer consultant. Marcel enjoys writing science fiction and fantasy and feels "reality and magic are intertwined in so many ways. Telling them apart is simply a matter of perspective."

Priscilla Galloway was born in Montreal. She has lived, written, taught, and scuba dived from the Pacific to the Atlantic, from southern farming country to northern mines, from the Caribbean to New Zealand. Her home base is Toronto. She has written eight picture books though she is now writing for an older audience, weaving strange visions of science fiction and fantasy around ancient tales.

James Alan Gardner lives in Kitchener, Ontario with his wife, Linda Carson. He divides his time between writing science fiction and producing computer textbooks. He won the 1989 Grand Prize in *Writers of the Future*, and has been published in *Amazing*, *Fantasy & Science Fiction*, and other science fiction magazines. His story, "Muffin Explains Teleology to the World at Large" won the Aurora Award for Best Work in English in 1991. He is also the author of two science fiction novels, *Expendable* and *Commitment Hour*.

Monica Hughes is the author of thirty novels – the majority of which are science fiction – as well as two picture books. She has won the Canada Council Prize (now the Governor General's Literary Award for Children's Text) twice. She first dreamed of writing at age ten, but didn't succeed until she began writing for young people in 1971 while living in Edmonton after stints in Ontario, England, Scotland, Zimbabwe, and Egypt. She loved reading the books of Jules Verne as a child, grew up with a mathematician father who was an amateur astronomer, and thinks the most exciting words in the English language are: What If . . .?

Jason Kapalka has been a grocery clerk, security guard, warehouse worker, short-order cook, vacuum cleaner salesman, and 'disgust' researcher. Jason Kapalka has had numerous stories published in *On Spec* magazine including "Frosty," the story appearing in this anthology. Originally from Edmonton, Alberta, he lives in California where he works for an internet game company.

Eileen Kernaghan grew up in the Okanagan Valley and has lived on the West Coast all her life. She has published four fantasy novels as well as numerous stories and poems, some of which have appeared in magazines such as *Tesseracts*, and anthologies such as *The Year's Best Fantasy and Horror*. Her young adult fantasy novel *Dance of the Snow Dragon* is, like "The Road to Shambhala," set in the mystical landscape of the Himalayas.

Alice Major, who currently lives in Edmonton, Alberta, has been fascinated by science fiction since she read *The Martian Chronicles* in grade eight. In addition, she has been writing poetry since grade four. It was inevitable, therefore, that sooner or later these two lifelong interests were going to merge. Alice Major has had poems published in many magazines throughout Canada and Britain. She has also published a fantasy novel for young readers called *The Chinese Mirror*.

Robert Priest is a poet, songwriter, playwright, and novelist who has performed his poems and songs on radio and TV. His rock videos are widely shown on MuchMusic and his songs have also been performed on *Sesame Street*. He won the Milton Acorn Memorial People's Poetry Award in 1989, and is the author of many books including *Ballad of the Blue Bonnet*,

Knights of the Endless Day, and *A Terrible Case of Stars*. Visit Robert Priest's website at www.interlog.com/~rpriest.

Jean-Louis Trudel lives in Montréal, Québec. He is the author of thirteen books and numerous short stories in both French and English, including the novel "Un trésor sur Serendib." He is the winner of the 1997 Aurora Award for Best Work in French for the short story "Lamente-toi, sagesse." He can live without television, sometimes without books, but never without writing.

Tim Wynne-Jones, as Amber Lightstone in his story, likes writing that is not about hiding things, but about discovering things. Speculative fiction is a great genre for someone like Tim, plagued with the 'What ifs?' But no single form of writing holds Tim's attention for long. He has written radio plays, opera librettos, lyrics for musicals, songs, picture books and novels. He has won the Governor General's Literary Award for Children's Text twice: in 1993 for *Some of the Kinder Planets* and in 1995 for *The Maestro*.